Moving on after a long-term marriage ends is killer and finding and decorating a new home is not something Alice enjoys. She's becoming annoyed with the inconveniences caused by those who are surveilling her and her new life. She is methodically putting her life back together, but when she finally begins to get her things in order, life throws her a curve ball no one could have seen coming.

A K'Anne Meinel novel

Also by K'Anne Meinel:

Novels in Paperback:

SHIPS *CompanionSHIP, FriendSHIP,*
RelationSHIP
Long Distance Romance
Children of Another Mother
Erotica
The Claim
Bikini's Are Dangerous
The Complete Series
Germanic
Malice Masterpieces 1
The First Five Books
Represented
Timed Romance
Malice Masterpieces 2
Books Six through Ten
The Journey Home
Out at the Inn
Shorts
Anthology Volume 1
Lawyered
Malice Masterpieces 3
Books Eleven through Fifteen
Blown Away
Blown Away
The Alternate Cover

Small Town Angel
Pirated Love
Doctored
Veil of Silence
Malice Masterpieces 4
Books Sixteen through Twenty
The Outsider
Pirated Heart
Recombinant Love
Survivors
Inn the Dog House
Flight
An Island Between Us
Malice Masterpieces 5
Books Twenty-One through Twenty-Five
Malice Masterpieces 6
Books Twenty-Six through Thirty
Beauty and the Beast

Vetted Series:
Vetted
Cavalcade (Prequel)
Pioneering (Prequel)
Vetted Further
Vetted Again

Novellas in Paperback:

Sapphic Surfer
Sapphic Cowgirl
Sapphic Cowboi
Sayyida
The Northwood Lodge

The Malice Series:
Mysterious Malice (Book 1)
Meticulous Malice (Book 2)
Mistaken Malice (Book 3)
Malicious Malice (Book 4)
Masterful Malice (Book 5)
Matrimonial Malice (Book 6)
Mourning Malice (Book 7)
Murderous Malice (Book 8)
Mental Malice (Book 9)
Menacing Malice (Book 10)
Minor Malice (Book 11)
Morally Malice (Book 12)
Morose Malice (Book 13)
Melancholy Malice (Book 14)

Mad Malice (Book 15)
Macabre Malice (Book 16)
Marinating Malice (Book 17)
Macerating Malice (Book 18)
Minacious Malice (Book 19)
Meddlesome Malice (Book 20)
Meandering Malice (Book 21)
Maniacal Malice (Book 22)
Monitoring Malice (Book 23)
Marked Malice (Book 24)
Mandating Malice (Book 25)
Methodical Malice (Book 26)
Malevolent Malice (Book 27)
Militarial Malice (Book 28)
Machiavellian Malice (Book 29)
Malefic Malice (Book 30)

Religious Experience
Lied

All Novels and Novellas in paperback are also available as e-books.

Novellas in Paperback Continued:

A Woman Down Under Series:
Shanghaied (Prequel)
Outback Born
Outback Bred
Outback Heritage
Outback Native
Outback Splendor
Outback Yearnings (Prequel)
Outback Escape

Pocket Paperbacks:
Mysterious Malice (Book 1)
Sapphic Surfer
Sapphic Cowgirl
Meticulous Malice (Book 2)
Mistaken Malice (Book 3)
Malicious Malice (Book 4)
Masterful Malice (Book 5)
Matrimonial Malice (Book 6)
Mourning Malice (Book 7)
Murderous Malice (Book 8)
Mental Malice (Book 9)
Menacing Malice (Book 10)
Minor Malice (Book 11)
Morally Malice (Book 12)
Morose Malice (Book 13)
Melancholy Malice (Book 14)
Mad Malice (Book 15)
Macabre Malice (Book 16)
Marinating Malice (Book 17)

In E-Book Format:
Short Stories
Fantasy
Wet & Wet Again
Family Night
Quickie ~ Against the Car
Quickie ~ Against the Wall
Quickie ~ Over the Couch
Mile High Club
Quickie ~ Under the Pier
Heel or Heal
Kiss
Family Night 2
Beach Dreams
Internet Dreamers
Snoggered
On the Parkway
Stable Affair
Kept
Stolen
Agitated
Love of my LIFE
Quickie in an Elevator, GOING DOWN?
Into the Garden
The Book Case
The Other Women
Menage a WHAT?

LARGE Print Novels
SHIPS CompanionSHIP, FriendSHIP, RelationSHIP
Erotica Volume 1
Long Distance Romance
Children of Another Mother
Bikini's Are Dangerous
The Complete Series
Malice Masterpieces
The First Five Books
To Love a Shooting Star
The Claim
Represented
Timed Romance

K'ANNE MEINEL

Methodical

Malice

ISBN-13: 978-1959436034

K'Anne Meinel is available for comments at KAnneMeinel@aim.com as well as on Facebook, Google +, or her blog @ http://kannemeinel.wordpress.com/ or on Twitter @ kannemeinelaim.com, or on her website @ www.kannemeinel.com if you would like to follow her to find out about stories and book's releases.

www.shadoepublishing.com

ShadoePublishing@gmail.com

Shadoe Publishing is a United States of America company
Cover by: K'Anne Meinel
Edited by: Deb Amia

Methodical Malice

PUBLISHER'S NOTE

METHODICAL MALICE

Book 26

Alice stared at Kathy in surprise. Why did she ask that question? Was she here to accuse Alice of causing Linda's death? "What do you want me to do about it?" she asked instead.

Kathy sighed gustily, obviously annoyed. She looked beyond Alice into the beach house and asked, "May I come in?"

Alice made a sweeping motion with her arm to indicate that her soon-to-be ex-wife was welcome to come in. She looked beyond Kathy at the Lexus parked in her driveway behind her Ferrari. The driveway was barely big enough for both cars and only if they were placed end to end. She glanced past them at the Pacific Coast Highway (PCH) where cars were speeding along a little too close for her comfort. Land was at such a premium down here in Malibu that they couldn't afford to waste any. She

glanced farther along the busy road to the now familiar car that was always parked there and always watching. Different people manned the vehicle in six- to eight-hour shifts, but someone was always watching, ready to follow if Alice went out. They no longer made any attempt to hide their presence, and Alice's Ferrari certainly wasn't inconspicuous. Closing the door firmly, she made sure the automatic lock engaged before turning to look at her wife, who was closely examining the small but expensive house.

Kathy looked around the ground floor. It was an open floor plan from front to back, the entrance only about five feet long by three feet wide. It led to a stairwell that curved upstairs, or you could bypass the stairwell and go directly into the living room. There was a modern gas fireplace along the wall and a few windows, so Alice could see along that side of her house. Bookshelves stood empty on each side of the bank of windows, nothing placed on them yet. The living room led into the dining area, which was furnished with only a cold, sterile, little table. If you turned to the left, you would enter a small kitchen, then a laundry area, and beyond that was a bedroom, probably intended for a maid. The kitchen, dining room, and bedroom areas all had French doors that led onto a balcony overlooking Malibu beach, which stretched the entire length of the relatively small house. The beach was filled with people.

But there was no warm, welcoming feeling in this house; even to Alice it felt bare. The townhome she'd had in the marina when she met Kathy had been sterile and impeccably clean, but at least there was furniture to indicate that someone lived there. This was too glacial. It reminded Kathy of a four-star hotel room. At least in a five-star hotel they supplied a bit of warmth. This was functional but just barely.

"Pass muster?" Alice asked, her sardonic question making her lips quiver as she hid a smile while watching her wife gaze about the rather insignificant house.

"Did you hear what I asked?" Kathy asked, clearly still upset.

Alice nodded and asked, "Did you hear what I asked?"

Kathy sighed, allowing an exasperated sound to escape from her nose for effect.

Alice was amused. She knew how to push Kathy's buttons.

"Did you kill her?"

Alice's expression didn't change. "No, I didn't."

"Do you know–?" Kathy began and then stopped in alarm as Alice determinedly advanced on her and grabbed her arm to propel her outside. When she tried to fight Alice off, twisting her arm to release it, Alice grabbed her again in a body hug that locked their bodies firmly together.

Shocked, Kathy stood still as Alice whispered in her ear, "My place is bugged. Say nothing," then she danced them through the remainder of the room and onto the back deck. She released Kathy as soon as they were both outside and she'd closed the patio door, a set of sliders helping it move effortlessly despite the sand. She continued to walk across the deck, down the steps, and onto the beach below.

Kathy stared at the back of her wife's head for a moment. She was still startled by how that whisper had made her shiver, and the feel of Alice's arms around her was a welcome comfort. She hadn't expected that, or her own reaction. She rubbed her arms, the warmth dissipating quickly on this cool fall day. She followed Alice down the steps to the beach.

Alice turned, confronting Kathy. "You can't say stuff like that."

"It's not like I knew your place was bugged. Who–?" she began.

"I'm not sure yet, but I assume it's the Feds. After what I gave the CIA, I'm certain they want more information from me." She didn't mention the car that was parked out along the PCH all the time. Kathy didn't need to know about that.

"Can't you remove them?"

"I don't have the equipment yet."

"Can you find out who–?" she began, and at Alice's expression the words died off. She realized she no longer had the right to ask about what happened in Alice's life.

"Look, I know you liked that woman and maybe even loved her–" Alice stopped, the pain of that statement hurt her, "but I didn't do what you asked, and I certainly am not going to investigate Linda's death."

"How do I know you aren't lying to me?"

"I don't lie to you, Kathy."

Kathy knew that was true. Alice might not tell her everything, but a direct question was always answered truthfully, at least Alice's version of the truth. She might be a killer, but she wasn't a liar. Kathy sighed again, exasperated as she looked away from her wife's startling and intriguing cat-like eyes. She looked back after a moment and asked, "Do you think it's legal for them to surveil you?"

Alice's eyebrow cocked in sardonic amusement at the question.

"Of course, it's not legal," Kathy sighed as she answered her own question, shrugged, and looked out at the fantastic view. She gestured at the house that was lacking in furniture and changed the subject. "Why haven't you decorated?"

Alice shrugged. "I didn't feel like it, and I didn't like the idea of having Sean draped on a couch." She shared a grin with her wife. Their son, a teenager with big feet, would stretch out on any surface and take it

over. "Besides, I only needed a bedroom for me and furniture for them." Her head nodded back towards the house and somehow included the children.

Kathy nodded. Alice had taken very little when she left their house, just her clothes and a few items from their home in Palos Verdes. She'd been very amenable during the divorce negotiations, going so far as giving Kathy more than the half she had asked for and was legally entitled to. Kathy had wondered about that. She knew there was probably a lot more in hidden assets, but she wasn't going to be greedy when Alice was being so generous. She turned away from Alice's inquiring eyes again. They seemed to look in her soul, and right now, she didn't want Alice looking there. Kathy gazed out at the crowds gathered on the beach despite the cool fall day. The view was beautiful, and the location ideal, even if the house was small. "Nice view," she commented.

Alice agreed with her, turning at the deliberate distraction to look out over the sands. "Yeah, it's a nice spot," she responded.

"The kids like it," Kathy agreed, having heard all about their other mother's house in Malibu. Kathy was just surprised it wasn't more elaborate. She looked up at the second story, interested in what the rest of the house looked like.

"Would you like a tour?" Alice asked, knowing her wife was curious and itching to see it all. She'd gotten this place for a song, relatively speaking, as some new wave kid singer with too much money, a busy career, and no time to live in the house, had sold it off.

"That would be nice," she admitted.

"Just be careful what you say," the blonde reminded her, waiting a moment for Kathy to nod her agreement.

Kathy followed as Alice led the way up to the back deck that spanned the length of the small cracker box house.

Alice showed her the rest of the downstairs. She was thinking that space alone would have been enough, if Alice didn't need bedrooms for the children. It was awkward for both women as Alice showed her the rest of the house in silence. The awkwardness was a new thing, something they had never really experienced except on a few memorable occasions in their married life.

Kathy could see that both kids' bedrooms were neatly made, and she knew that neither Sean nor Emily would have left them in that condition. There wasn't much in the rooms other than basic furniture. Most of their things were kept at the house in Palos Verdes, where they had lived almost all their lives. Neither of them remembered the house at the marina. And that reminded her, "Kit is coming home this weekend."

Alice looked up as she exited the bathroom situated between the two kids' bedrooms. She was heading into the master bedroom that traversed almost the entire length of the back of the house and overlooked the beach. The master had its own private, rather elaborate bathroom, one of the main reasons she had bought this home. "I'd like to see her," Alice reminded her wife as she allowed her to walk into the bedroom.

"I'll make sure she knows that," Kathy said as she looked at the walk-in closet and the inviting bathroom with the jetted tub, separate shower, skylights, toilet, and bidet. She spotted something on the floor near the French patio doors on the far side of the king-sized bed. It was a nightgown, and it wasn't anything Alice would wear. Her heart twisted painfully as she realized Alice must already be seeing someone else. She hardened her heart against that thought, knowing it was really none of her business. "She's declared her major."

"Oh, yeah?" Alice asked, intrigued. She had been aware of the exact moment when Kathy saw that nightgown, something she had deliberately left on the floor where it had been thrown. She carefully schooled her face not to smile at the game she was playing. She wasn't certain that the bugs that were listening in didn't also have video, but she would have to check that out soon. Inwardly, she sighed. If *they* would just leave her alone, she would leave them alone; however, who *they* were was yet to be determined.

Kathy turned to look at Alice, her back to the French doors. She had seen that the doors afforded Alice an even better view of Malibu Beach, the second story providing a grander perspective than any of the one-story homes. "You aren't going to like her choice."

"No?" Alice inquired, her eyebrow cocking in inquiry.

Kathy smiled slightly as she spoke with her wife, her child's second mother since she was eight years old. Alice had saved her then, had saved them both from a life she couldn't even contemplate now. "She's decided to go into law enforcement."

Kathy was surprised when Alice began to laugh. The blonde laughed so hard that tears ran from the corners of her eyes, and she wiped them away as she continued to chuckle.

"May I ask why that is so funny?"

"It's just ironic, don't you think?" Alice used the sleeve of her blouse to dry the tears, still sniggering.

Kathy had to smile as she nodded too. It *was* ironic, considering all the crimes Alice had committed over the years. Fortunately, their children didn't know, at least, *they didn't know much*, she mentally amended. She recalled that Emily knew a little more than she needed to and had asked a couple leading questions, obviously curious about what she had overheard

and nearly spouting information in front of a cop. She remembered that Linda was the cop Emily had nearly said too much in front of, and she was now dead. She'd come here to ask Alice about that, at least that had been the premise of her visit. She made to move back through the room and go downstairs. "I'll tell her to stop by," Kathy promised as she reached the stairs. She glanced at the bare walls, the color a boring, muted off-white. "You really should decorate. Maybe get some furniture? A TV?" She noted the game set up in the room that was dedicated to Sean had a computer, and the multi-colored light-up keyboard was apparently only for games. Alice's small office off the master bedroom didn't even have a desk, much less the many computers Alice had used so often in the past. It was curious to Kathy that there was no computer equipment after all this time since Alice had bought the house and moved in. There was no lived-in feeling to the place, and there was obviously no work being done here. What did Alice do with her days? Kathy remembered the nightgown and tried not to think of what Alice did with her nights. Then, she remembered that Alice didn't need to confine those activities to nights.

"Yeah, maybe Kit and the kids would like to help me?" she offered.

"I'll mention it. I'm sure Sean will try to talk you into more computer games," she commented wryly, knowing their son well. It was a good thing his grades were up to snuff, or those games would be locked up. She would stay on top of that.

"I think I have enough," she gestured through the open door of the boy's room where the elaborate gaming system was set up.

"Is that original?" Kathy asked, looking a second time. She'd missed it the first time she glanced in the room as she was focused more on the well-made bed. The computer games were stacked neatly on a table near a very wide monitor, and two gaming chairs allowed the users to lean back from

the floor as they played. She saw now, there were several gaming consoles hooked up to multiple screens.

"The Nintendo?" Alice confirmed, grinning as she nodded at the game that came out in the 1980s. "Yeah, I kicked his ass on that. He is so used to the modern graphics and doodads that he never saw me coming in Super Mario Bros with all the hidden mushrooms and whatnots."

Kathy laughed. She'd forgotten that Alice liked that game. "But what about Duck Hunt?" she teased as she left the doorway and headed for the stairs once again.

"Oh, yeah. Em and I enjoyed that, and it annoyed Sean, so bonus," she teased back, knowing her son had been put out that his younger sister had beaten him at the hand-eye coordination of the simple game. The games he had now were so much more sophisticated, and a lot of them involved war, which simply didn't interest Alice as it might once have.

They proceeded down the stairs to the front door, and Kathy noted that the alarm system wasn't something Alice would have permitted in their own home. It didn't seem as sophisticated, but maybe she wasn't reading it right? Something was afoot here, and although she was curious about it, she wasn't going to ask. It wasn't her place, and while she still cared for Alice, it was obvious the blonde had moved on. She swallowed again, wondering who belonged to the nightgown upstairs.

"I'll tell Kit to give you a call when she's settled in the house, so you two can make plans," Kathy promised as she headed out to her blue Lexus. She glanced at the flashy Ferrari Alice now drove, something that had surprised her after all the Porsches the blonde had owned during their years together. She looked up in surprise and found a woman barring her way. Kathy looked at her curiously, wondering if this was the mysterious

nightgown owner, then dismissing that thought immediately. This woman was not Alice's type. She was dressed very conservatively in a suit.

"Hello, Alice," the woman said, ignoring Kathy. She knew who Kathy was from the pictures they had of Alice's family. She was a nobody and a mouse compared to Alice Weaver. The suited woman still wondered what sort of woman could have held Alice Weaver's attention for all those years. There had to be something more to her if Alice had married her. She knew from their surveillance of Alice that a divorce had been filed. Several of their team wondered if they could use that to their benefit. After all, a wife couldn't testify against her spouse but an ex-wife could.

"Hello, Madelyn," Alice responded in an amused tone that irritated both Madelyn and Kathy. Kathy was curious to know who this was, and seeing that curiosity and being courteous, Alice introduced them. "Madelyn Korbel, this is my ex-wife, Kathy."

The two women eyed each other. Madelyn dismissed the mousy woman, and Kathy asked, "CIA?" in a tone that left them both with no doubt that she despised the acronym and the people behind it.

Madelyn was intrigued. Why would Alice's ex-wife care if she was with the CIA or not? She nodded, a bit coldly in agreement.

Kathy was feeling hurt by Alice referring to her as her ex-wife. The paperwork wasn't final yet. Her tone when she replied was perhaps a bit touchy.

"Whatcha want, Madelyn?" Alice asked, leaning against the wall of the house in a relaxed slouch and watching the two women. She was wondering if Madelyn frequently underestimated people. She could see how dismissive she was being of Kathy. If she only knew....

"Is there somewhere we could talk?" Madelyn asked, glancing at the beach house before them curiously.

Alice nodded and held her hand out to Kathy. "Maybe you should come back in for this?" she offered.

"This is private," Madelyn stated, glancing at the mousy woman again and reassessing her. Her tone brooked no argument, but Alice chose to ignore it.

"Yeah, but whether I tell her later or she hears it first-hand, she is going to want to know," Alice pointed out.

"You mean she knows–?"

Alice nodded. "I didn't keep anything from her."

Madelyn looked at the two women again. She was surprised and trying to hide it. It didn't pay to let your emotions or feelings show around people like this. She tried to shrug it off, acting as though it didn't matter as she followed Kathy into the house. She was looking about just as curiously as Kathy had and noting how bare things were.

"Let's go out on the deck," Alice offered. "Anyone want anything to drink?" she asked as she gestured towards the back door.

"This isn't something we want overheard," Madelyn warned as Alice went to get three glasses from the cupboard and the pitcher of lemonade she kept in the fridge.

"I understand that, Madelyn; however, I would prefer to go *out on the deck*," the blonde said meaningfully, staring Madelyn down until she caught on. It didn't take long for the CIA operative to begin glancing around. She wondered where the bugs could possibly be hidden. There wasn't much furniture or decorations to hide them.

When they were settled on the deck and sipping ice-cold lemonade with real lemon slices floating in the glasses, Madelyn settled back in her chair and sighed. The cool fall day here was still much warmer than back east. Langley often seemed cold, but perhaps, it was the buildings. Then,

thinking about the work that went on there and the people, she realized it was probably the atmosphere of the place. She looked up at the sun, relishing what little warmth it provided.

"Going to sunbathe later?" Alice asked, the sarcasm obvious as she watched the eastern woman with her nose pointed towards the sun and her eyes closed.

"I wish I had the time," she admitted with a smile.

"I'm sure you would like to get down to business then," Alice hinted subtly.

Madelyn smiled. That was something she liked about Alice; she didn't bullshit around like so many people. "You knew they were going to want more," she began.

Alice nodded, an enigmatic smile hovering around her lips as she sipped delicately at her lemonade. "We had an agreement–" she started.

"And we intend to honor it. We do, however, need more from you."

"What's in it for me?"

"Alice, there are over a dozen Russian nationals from very prominent families that are dead, and we need to get information on them."

"I gave you a lot of that information," she pointed out dryly.

"And we need to know how you got that information and how much more you have."

"What has that got to do with me?"

They stared at each other. Alice was looking innocent. She'd had years of practice at that, and Madelyn's eyes narrowed as she watched the woman and wondered how she had gotten away with so much for so long. She'd seen a lot of the redacted reports…hell, she'd written many of them. Director Wolf had been frustrated to learn the complete reports weren't available to him as he'd assumed they would be since the redacted reports

didn't tell him everything he needed to know about Alice Weaver. The FBI's paperwork was even worse than the CIA's, and it frustrated and intrigued the agents more than it should have. Alice Weaver seemed like an ordinary citizen, but the four-inch file on her led to various operations over the years where some of their players had disappeared. Some reports only implied that she was involved, and other reports blatantly stated her name, but her role in these affairs wasn't clear. There was much speculation and conjecture, but proof was non-existent in most of their information. There was nothing they could pin on her, especially after the latest release of information had absolved her from prosecution. Still, some of their best agents had been put on the job to *try*.

"Alice we both know there is more information–" she began, gesturing with her hand and feeling suddenly inadequate. It was just like when she first started out with the agency and people like Alice could have danced rings around her. She'd been so naive. Why Alice Weaver still make her feel that way after all these years…she had no idea.

"We do?" Alice toyed with her prey. Suddenly tired of the game, she asked, "Should I have Nia Toyomoto contact you?"

"Why would you need your lawyer?" she asked, suddenly alert. If Alice was lawyering up so quickly, there must be more…there had to be a lot more. She knew from several sources how close they had come to that information ending up on the evening news. The little bits that Alice had fed the press had put several prominent reporters on the trail, and it was up to the CIA to keep the press from away from the information for the sake of national security. Even now, deals were being cut with reporters, TV stations, and powerful men and women to keep the information away from the public.

"Do I? I was under the impression that I had immunity from prosecution?" she confirmed, and at Madelyn's reluctant nod she added, "I gave you plenty of information."

"That my teams are going over with a fine-tooth comb. You knew that."

Alice smiled congenially, taking another sip of her lemonade for effect. "And?"

"That's just the tip of the iceberg...."

"Really?" Alice asked, sounding intrigued.

"What can I offer you as an incentive?"

"Nothing." Alice replied with a note of finality. She gestured to the expensive beach house they were sitting behind. "But you can call your dogs off."

"My dogs?" Madelyn asked, intrigued.

"Your people aren't watching my house and bugging me?"

"Not yet," she assured her, suddenly amused and yet...*not*. If someone had authorized surveillance on this woman, she wanted to know why and who. Alice was prickly enough as it was. If she thought she was being surveilled, it wouldn't bode well for those involved. *Maybe someone at the FBI*...her thoughts trailed off, but that should have been authorized by their joint task team, which she was heading up.

Alice tried to stare her down, but Madelyn was good at this game too, and she wouldn't be intimidated. She had answered honestly, and that seemed to ingratiate her to Alice. The blonde believed her but that led to the obvious question: Who was surveilling her? "You got a name for me yet?" she asked, changing the subject quickly before she became angry over this information.

"No," Madelyn admitted, quickly adding, "but I am working on it, and I hope to have it for you soon."

"That's not good enough, Madelyn," Alice said, her voice changing to a warning tone that they both knew the agent might want to heed.

"I understand, and I am working on it. At the same time, if you could—"

"Not another name. Not another tidbit of information," Alice assured her, draining her glass. "Turnabout is fair play. You know that."

Madelyn did know that, but she had had to try. Director Wolf and others didn't understand that you just didn't demand information from people like Alice Weaver. She amended that comment in her mind. *You didn't demand anything from Alice Weaver.* Already, they were trying to find a work-around to the immunity from prosecution paperwork. Those dead men that Alice had handed them were important Russian men. They were related in different ways: some through business and others through what they believed were mafia ties. "How do those men relate to the arms sale?" Madelyn asked. The agents were still trying to put the pieces of the puzzle together.

Alice just sat there with her empty glass in her hand and watched her prey. If Madelyn wanted more information from her, she was going to have to offer more. Getting the dismissal of prosecution from the federal government, the local police, and the IRS hadn't been easy, but it had worked out in her favor. The men she had given the authorities the extensive information on—Vashti Baltizar, Leonid Baltizar, Alexander or Xander Baltizar, the Bogomolov family, Filipov, and Kozlov—were very bad men. Their business ties had seemed obvious, and they were all part of The Assemblage, a crime syndicate of massive, international

proportions. If the CIA hadn't discovered that yet with the information Alice had given them, they soon would.

Madelyn felt decidedly uncomfortable. Alice didn't often play games, but when she did, she played better than most people. Her games usually ended with someone dead, and Madelyn knew that the blonde hid her tracks very well. The redacted paperwork was filled with assumptions but few hard facts that showed Alice Weaver was a killer in the various cases Madelyn and others had worked on. In Madelyn's private thoughts, even the ones she dared to carefully word and put into writing, Alice was a serial killer of proportions they had never seen before, but Madelyn's opinions didn't matter in the greater scheme of things, and they didn't contribute to what she was trying to achieve.

"I'll be in town for a few days, if you want to talk to me," Madelyn told her, reaching into her suit for a card. She noted Alice shifted in her chair, prepared for any movement on Madelyn's part that might be construed as an attack. Only an experienced operative would note that minuscule shift in body movement that placed Alice in a position to defend herself. She admired that about the woman even as she unconsciously acknowledged her fear and how dangerous this woman really was. "That's my new cell number. You can call it anytime." Instead of handing her the card, she slid it across the table.

"Thank you," Alice said politely, not picking up the card as she watched Madelyn. She was polite, but she wasn't going to add anything to that statement and give her old acquaintance one iota more information. She was still owed some things, and until she got them, she wasn't giving away anything more.

Madelyn sighed inwardly. She had told Alice the truth. They were working on getting that name for her as promised, but with everything

Alice had given them, their resources on the investigations were stretched thin. Still, she knew she better produce something and quickly.

Alice led her to the front door and closed it behind her when she left, returning quickly to the deck. Kathy was standing and asked, "What was that about?"

"A fishing expedition," she stated blandly, glancing at the embossed card curiously and putting it in her pocket for future use. She would call it at some point. She deserved information, and Madelyn knew what might happen if she had to wait much longer for it. The meeting, while relatively short, hadn't produced anything that was of use to the agent.

"I better be going," Kathy stated. She wondered why Alice had asked her to stay for that meeting. She was relieved to learn the woman wasn't anyone who was involved with her wife, but it concerned her that the CIA was still calling on her. "I'll have Kat call you," she reminded her.

"Thanks, I'd appreciate that," Alice responded, stopping outside the door to watch Kathy get in the Lexus and back out carefully into the parking lane, then merge smoothly onto the highway, the powerful engine of the Lexus making it look effortless. She waved and then pushed a button once she got inside, closing the gate this time. She had left it open earlier. She glanced only briefly at the car parked across the highway.

* * * * *

"She wouldn't give me anything," Madelyn confirmed as she talked on her car phone using her Bluetooth speaker.

"Then you have to squeeze her," Director Wolf told her.

Madelyn nearly laughed aloud in his ear. He underestimated Alice Weaver, and he had no idea who he was messing with. Alice Weaver

pissed off and irritated was just what she didn't need. She hadn't missed the underlying menace in Alice's tone that told her she better find the person who had arranged things against Alice. She had to find a name, and it better be a good one, or Alice might direct her anger towards Madelyn. She didn't need that headache, and she'd really like to live a good, long life. Why had she come back to the agency...for this?

"We really need more out of her. This whole thing was handled sloppily. There should have been more time. You can't blackmail the CIA," he insisted.

And yet, Alice Weaver had blackmailed them, thought Madelyn, *and very handily.* Using the media, the unofficial fourth branch of the government, against the government had been brilliant, something she had admired about the prickly woman. She thought back to one of the many meetings they'd had in the last couple months since Alice had given them the memory card with the information on the Russian mafia members, oligarchs that unofficially ran the country.

"We should obtain warrants and raid this Alice Weaver's house," one agent had contended hotly at one of their many meetings on the subject.

"She's immune to that by our own paperwork," another defended her, perhaps admiringly, as he slapped at the letter that freed one Alice Weaver from prosecution in return for information she had supplied the CIA. The way the paperwork was worded, even the FBI, who they had shared information with, couldn't go after Alice.

"She can't possibly cuckhold us like this," another argued, feeling bitter that *anyone* could blackmail them.

"Don't be too overconfident about our bureau's procedures," Madelyn reminded them. "There are reasons they are put into place for situations such as this.

"Your department is responsible for this," an FBI agent allowed to sit in on the meeting put in testily.

"Careful, there," Madelyn warned him. "We are responsible for this mess, and as we dig deeper, we are learning that some of it is of our own making. The FBI had some of this information," she gestured to the piles of data they had compiled, "but not to the extent we have been supplied," she indicated the mass of paperwork that had resulted from their investigation of the information Alice provided. It was being divided up by the names she gave them, and still there were gaping holes in it all, which they knew was due to other names being omitted. The odd footage they had seen of some sort of explosion in Kazakhstan was still not explained, but the pictures showing American weapons with the same Kazakhstan background were obvious. "Before pointing fingers and assigning blame, we should figure out who all these people are," she gestured to the bios they already had on each of the players, but these were still being added to as each one was investigated more thoroughly. They were hampered by these people being Russian citizens, and they had to rely on operatives working and living there as well as sleeper agents, who couldn't reveal where they were getting their information.

"There is exculpatory evidence—" began one agent, trying to get the conversation back to Alice's apparent involvement in the deaths of these men.

"We already know that Alice Weaver was held in prison with Sasha Brenhov. Of course, there will be fingerprints and other evidence, and some of it will have been planted by our Russian friends," another agent pointed out.

The endless debates over the evidence were frustrating to some and fascinating to others as they all worked to make sense of the information.

"We should go after Sasha Brenhov. She emerged unscathed from all of this," someone else put in. "Isn't she married to an American citizen?"

"No, they aren't married, but she did leave her assets to the woman. I hear that firm in New York is still straightening out the legal entanglements of that. Sasha Brenhov's assets are rather extensive."

"She didn't lose anything due to her supposed death."

"You'll have a helluva time if you go after her without proof, and you will be swarmed by teams of lawyers. She's a Russian national, for Christ's sake!"

"There are errors in how the agency went about investigating Alice Weaver," the FBI agent pointed out, bringing them back to the point they were here to discuss.

"Are you trying to lay blame at our feet again?" Wolf asked as he came in, proving he had been listening to their endless debates regarding the investigation.

"No, sir, but there are procedures set in place to avoid–" he began.

"Then put them in your report," Wolf told the man, shutting him up. He handed Madelyn a pile of paperwork he had scooped up on his way through the computer department where they were still trying to figure out why they were having computer problems. They had determined the issues arrived at the same time as Alice Weaver's information, but they couldn't prove that she had planted a virus. This virus was completely different from the one wending its way through the various police departments in California. There was something insidious about all these security breaches. The FBI and the CIA had systems that prevented people from breaking in from the outside. There were certain parts that could not be accessed from external computer consoles, and yet, both agencies had hiccups in their systems that shouldn't be there. The

computer geeks were working overtime trying to figure it out. Just when they fixed one glitch, another would pop up in some completely unrelated system. It was exasperating and made no sense. Things like this did not happen with their computer systems. "This one is a simple children's game," he indicated the report that showed some sort of Pac-Man game eating data within a financial program.

"This doesn't make sense," Madelyn murmured, looking at the readouts. It was a familiar and frustrating refrain from those involved in the investigation of the computer viruses.

"Are you sure she didn't plant–?" Wolf began, but Madelyn cut him off.

"I'm sure she planted something as a distraction, but your men already wiped those from the system," she pointed out.

"There has to be a way for us to get warrants and monitor her computer systems to get the information we need…" he began, just as determined as the other agents on the teams to get more out of Alice Weaver and figure out if the virus they had found on her disk was planted deliberately.

"Yes, sir, but we have to prove intent, and it's just not here," another agent pointed out, waving to the paperwork. "We can monitor her. We don't need a judge to sign off on that, but what would that prove? She has money, that was proven by the IRS, but they can't go after it now."

"Wouldn't FISA (the Foreign Intelligence Surveillance Act) come into play since Russia is involved?" another agent asked.

"FISA is only used to target foreign spies and terrorists. Alice Weaver is an American citizen," Madelyn pointed out, proving she was paying attention to the many conversations going on around her. "Furthermore, we'd have to get a special court to grant approval to operate in secret and

do wiretaps, and she's already protected by *that*," she indicated the paperwork that Alice had signed before she gave them the disk.

"But Sasha Brenhov is a Russian citizen," someone else pointed out.

"And Sasha doesn't live in the United States. We can investigate, and if we find she did something that affects America's interests, we could ask to have her extradited, but Russia will never approve that, and our own country wouldn't ask," Wolf pointed out. "However, compiling information on that businesswoman is a good idea."

And so, the debates continued for months as they sifted through all the fact and fiction they had gathered. One thing no one had noticed immediately was that each of the dead people, despite their power and seeming wealth while alive, had left behind no money on their deaths. Their families, if they had any, essentially inherited nothing. There was a money trail between the mafia members, but no one in the FBI or CIA realized that none of those people had any money left following their deaths and immediately prior to their sudden departures from this world.

"Madelyn do you think you might go out to Los Angeles and visit our offices there? You could talk to her and find out what these photos mean," Wolf asked, indicating the pictures that had obviously been taken from drones and showed the Kazakhstan landscape and American military equipment.

"Yes, I can do that, but you know she won't give us anything more. We still haven't fulfilled our agreement to her."

"How is that aspect of the investigation going?" he asked, not really caring if they ever satisfied their obligation to Alice Weaver. *Something about her–.*

"Still all dead ends," she told him, cutting off his thoughts, "but something stinks, and eventually, my people will figure it out." She knew

she was obligated to keep him informed, and he would have to be told if her people eventually figured it out, but that didn't mean she wouldn't fulfil the terms of their agreement with Alice.

* * * * *

"Mom!" an exuberant, younger version of Kathy launched herself into Alice's welcoming arms.

"Wow! Look at you, all collegiate and shit," Alice said drolly when she had Kit at arm's length. The smile on Alice's features was genuine. She loved this kid, even if she wasn't blood. She'd endeared herself to the older woman's heart many years ago.

Kit grinned down at Alice. She had never realized how truly petite Alice was. She hadn't gained back all the weight she lost, and she looked…tired and quite a bit older. This worried the young woman briefly as she entered the beach house followed by her younger siblings.

"Mind if I go up to my room?" her son asked respectfully.

"Homework done?" Alice asked, knowing he only wanted to play on the computers. The games were top of the line, and she'd played them too. Ostensibly, she was using them to familiarize herself with the games, but she had used them to send a few messages that wouldn't be monitored, since she was so closely watched right now. She'd have to do something about that soon.

"Yes, Mom, and they don't assign homework over Thanksgiving," Sean reminded her as he started up the stairs.

Alice blinked. It was Thanksgiving already? How'd she missed that one? She looked at Emily, standing there and watching her. "We have got

to decorate this place," the young girl instructed her, parroting her other mother.

"Why don't we all plan to go shopping on Saturday?" Alice asked, including Sean, who had just reached the top of the stairs.

"Can we get a TV?" he called down.

"Yes, for each room," she called back.

"Yay!" he said excitedly and hurried into his room to fire up the computer games. He would call his friends and ask them about the best TVs. He was certain they would have all the latest information he would need, and he was confident he could talk Alice into buying them.

"Why Saturday?" Emily asked as she watched Kit examining the sparse furnishings.

"Shopping on Black Friday would kill me," Alice told her blandly. "The deals will still be there Saturday, and you two can start shopping for Christmas." She put her arm around her daughter, hugging her close. "What are you going to get me?"

Emily chuckled appreciatively and looked again at Kit, who was watching them both now. She was amazed at how much her little sister was finally growing and how much her eye shape was becoming like Alice's. There was something different about Em's eye color though. It seemed to have changed since she was a child.

"Look at you two, like two peas in a pod. Hang on! I want a picture of this," Kit said, warning them to stand still while she held up her phone to snap a shot. When she had taken three pictures in rapid succession, she smiled down at the result. You could see the family resemblance in these two, and yet, when she stood next to Emily, Kit thought she looked just like her too. How the hell was that possible? She'd never considered how her birth mother, Kathy, had become pregnant with her siblings. Had she

carried Alice's eggs? How the heck was it possible for Emily to look like both their mothers?

The three of them spent an enjoyable afternoon together, and Sean only came down to raid the refrigerator for food, lamenting loudly about the healthy stuff Alice had filled it with. They determined that Alice must come to dinner since Kathy had extended the offer. The women might be divorcing, but that didn't mean they weren't still a family. It was soothing to Alice's ears to listen to the girls chatting about college and life in general. Emily's ambitions weren't as defined as the older college student's yet. This was family. It was familiar, and she loved it.

She moved them outside after listening to Sean's complaints about 'no food' after his second and third excursions to the fridge for snacks, and he left them to their conversation.

"So, what's this I hear about law enforcement?" she smiled at Kit over the lemonade they were sipping. Emily had slipped down to the beach to check out who was about. She was looking for celebrities she could tell her friends she had seen. Both Sean and Emily's friends were salivating over an invite to their mom's new digs.

"Are you disappointed?" Kit asked, a little defensive.

"Nope, not in the least. Are you?" Alice asked, waiting for her response. She was a very patient cat and mouse player, much more so than this daughter, who was bound to her only by the bonds of love. She saw so much of Kathy in this young woman when she thought back to their college days. She'd had no romantic interest in Kathy at that time. Kathy had just been part of a group of young women that her sister hung out with.

"I'm excited about my courses again. It was becoming tedious," Kit admitted. "But that was good advice to get the basics out of the way.

Now, I can concentrate on the fun courses. They aren't easy, but they are truly fascinating."

Alice smiled, showing off her new, neat, straight smile. Her teeth had been bad for so long after the torture and other hardships she endured, and she was pleased they were fixed now and no longer caused her pain. Going back to her Los Angeles dentist had proven to be a good idea. He fixed what others had changed about her smile. "Have you decided what area of law enforcement you are going into?" Alice asked carefully, not wishing to offend her daughter or cause her antennae to rise.

"I'm not going to be a cop," she said with a self-deprecating grin. "From what I've heard, I think this family has had enough of that." She waited a moment before adding, "I think I'll get my master's degree, so I can enter higher on the food chain wherever I land. Maybe Internal Affairs, so I can go after dirty cops."

Alice was surprised, and that didn't happen often. Kathy must have kept their daughter well informed…then she looked at her other daughter on the beach chatting with someone, and her eyes narrowed slightly. She thought maybe she knew who had kept Kit well informed. She only hoped that Emily never shared the whole story with anyone; that would be unfortunate. She looked back at Kit and something else occurred to her. With a master's in law enforcement and the ensuing courses, this kid, who studied hard, would probably get top grades and come to the attention of other law enforcement people. Suddenly, she wondered if Madelyn knew of Kit's plans. People might come calling from the FBI, the CIA, and other less desirable acronyms. That was the part that worried her. "That's a good idea," she said, not discouraging the young woman. She knew Kit had delayed declaring her major for as long as she could. Now, the

master's program would keep her in school at least two more years. "Are you going to stay at Stanford?"

"I was thinking of transferring to Harvard for my master's," she informed Alice, watching her carefully for any sign of displeasure. For some reason, she had always wanted to please this woman. Alice had been extremely supportive of everything she wanted to do, not just financially but also providing emotional and informational support, anything Kit needed. She had to admit that meeting Alice had been the best thing that could have happened to her and her mother. Alice had provided them a level of financial stability they had never previously experienced. Even during the time her mother had been missing and was thought dead, Alice had been there for them all. Remembering her own brush with the insidious, she knew Alice had somehow protected her. She could see by the ravages on Alice's face and body that her time away from their family hadn't been pleasant, but she wouldn't pry. Just as she hadn't asked her mother why she was going through with the divorce while seemingly mourning the death of their marriage. It was obvious, at least to their children, that these two women loved each other.

"Want me to write letters?" Alice asked, not telling the young woman she could get her in with no effort at all. She was pleased that Kit wanted to go to her mother's and her alma mater.

"When I'm ready," she admitted. "I still have to get my bachelor's degree." She sighed inwardly, not sure why it had been so stressful to tell Alice her plans. Her mother hadn't objected in any way, and for that Kit was immensely relieved.

"Maybe I should consider Yale too? You know, have a back-up plan?" she teased Alice and enjoyed a good laugh at her mother's expense. She

went on to talk about her roommates, and when she mentioned a guy named John, Alice's antennae perked up.

"How close are you and John becoming?" she asked casually...perhaps too casually.

"It's just a college thing for now," Kit admitted, sounding so grown up. "I told him I can't do serious. I want to get my degrees first."

Alice smiled slightly. *Atta girl*, she thought. "You still need to have fun," she pointed out. "Don't become so serious that you neglect your personal life away from academia." She felt like a hypocrite saying that. That was *exactly* what she wanted for their little girl, who was all grown up now. Still, her heart squeezed as she was reminded of Kathy at a younger age again when Kit smiled. *Study. Don't go out with guys. Get your degree and keep your nose to the grindstone*, is what she thought. Still, she had to be the parent, and encouraging her daughter to have a fully rounded life was the right thing to do. She sighed. She hated being a parent sometimes.

"Oh, I do," and Kit launched into stories of going to parties on beaches up in the San Francisco Bay area. Some of the stories were repeats of earlier stories she had told for Alice and Emily's benefit.

Alice had deliberately kept those conversations on tape in the house for the benefit of whoever was bugging her place. She reminded herself she would have to take care of that soon. She kept telling herself that there were a few things she had to take care of. It was *time*.

The visit was going well, and Alice was contemplating ordering pizza for everyone when Kit mentioned Emily's friend, Carmen. "I don't like that chick," Kit mentioned. "There is something insidious about her. She is always listening where she doesn't belong."

Alice's eyes narrowed slightly at this. It was odd to have someone else confirm her feelings. She had never liked that friend of Emily's either. She inwardly sighed, knowing she should have done something about it a while ago. She remembered meeting Carmen's parents, Sandi and Richard Pasternack. They were neighbors of theirs in Palos Verdes. They had triggered several red flags in her psyche. She couldn't discount the fact that Sandi worked for Sebastian. That on its own told her a lot about the woman, but it was the look in that woman's eyes that had set off all her alarms. That was something else she would have to investigate.

"Wasn't that girl one of the mean girls that Emily always complained about?" Kit mused, not expecting an answer.

Alice thought about that. The girl's attitude towards her sickly daughter had changed abruptly with Alice's return. Was that deliberate? Had her parents put her up to it? She remembered very well looking in Sandi Pasternack's eyes and seeing like for like. Then, seeing Sandi at Sebastian's house had been a shock to them both, which reminded her that she hadn't seen a death notice for Sebastian. She should visit him. God! What was wrong with her? She hadn't been taking care of business, and that would have to change. She looked out at the rapidly fading sunlight and saw her younger daughter heading back up the beach. She enjoyed the sight of her daughter's rapidly growing frame, which was finally filling out. It was as though Mother Nature was catching up for the times when she was so ill. Emily wasn't the skeleton she had been then, although she still needed to pack on some pounds. But then, so did Alice.

"Would you like me to order pizza? You can eat while we decide which stores to hit on Saturday?" Alice asked Kit.

"Sounds good. I want a vegan pizza please, if you don't mind?"

"Vegan? Since when?" Alice asked, amused.

"I love its cracker thin crust," she admitted. "Vegan or even vegetarian is healthier." She sounded sanctimonious, like a lot of college kids who thought of themselves as smarter than their parents.

Alice smiled. She'd have to agree. "I do recall a kid who once had extra meat on her meat lover's pizza," she pointed out as she reached for her phone. She already knew Sean's preferences for extra everything, and she would get a whole pie just for him and his voracious appetite. She could hear him on the video game upstairs as she hadn't bought headphones for it. As Emily walked up, she asked, "Em what do you want on your pizza?" just as Kit was enthusiastically denying her past love of meat lover's pizza.

"You know I love Hawaiian deep dish," Em said with a smile, showing the need for a bit of orthodontia in that smile. Alice made a mental note to discuss that with Kathy.

"There's a restaurant down here that adds pineapple and cherries on the pizza," Alice told her as she punched up the number on her phone.

"That doesn't sound…good," Emily stated hesitantly.

"Oh, it is. I promise," Alice told her as the person answered, and she placed orders for three pies plus plenty of soda and bread sticks. She had her credit card memorized, and the order was soon completed. "They'll be here within the hour," she informed her daughters.

"But cherries?" Emily whined, continuing the conversation now that her mother was off the phone.

"Remember how much you loved the ham at Easter with the pineapple and cherries your mom fastened to the sides with toothpicks?" Alice reminded the youth of those traditional meals Kathy had engineered. She was grateful for the memories and grateful that Kathy had given her a

night alone with the children, even if Sean was glued to his video games and not really participating.

"Oh, yeah," she put in, suddenly brightening at the memory of that food and occasion. Pineapple on pizza had once seemed gross, but she had wanted to like the same things as Momma A, a moniker they had assigned to Alice years ago, and Alice liked Hawaiian pizza. Cherries didn't sound quite as gross now.

"You will love the pizza on the east coast if you like crackers for crusts," Alice continued, picking up where she'd left off in her conversation with Kit. They continued discussing food and the possibility of Kit going east for school at Harvard.

"Do you know what you want to be when you grow up?" Kit asked Emily.

"I hate the phrase 'when I grow up!' It isn't like you are so grown up." Emily stated to her older sister. "I've seen some adults that never grew up," she pointed out.

"Touché," Alice murmured, amused.

Kit laughed. "You do have a point."

"I don't know what I want to do yet." She looked at Alice and asked, "What do you want me to be?"

"Happy," Alice answered without any hesitation.

"No, really, Mom," she said, aggrieved. "What would you like me to become?"

Alice leaned forward and took her daughter's hand in her own, squeezing it slightly. As a woman known for not being very demonstrative, both her daughters were touched by this gesture in completely different ways. "I want you to be healthy and happy," she answered softly. "It's getting cold out here. Let's go inside. We can

decide where we are going shopping and compose a list of what I need while we wait for our pizza."

Kit grinned ruefully, seeing how her actions had unnerved her mother, or so she imagined. Emily swelled with undisguised pride over what Alice said. The three of them went inside to wait for their pizza, and the two younger women started a list for Alice. It was going to be a very expensive weekend.

* * * * *

"Thank you for inviting me," Alice told Kathy as she helped put the trimmings on the table. They had inserted extra leaves in the table just for this occasion. They'd already discussed Emily's orthodontia, and Kathy was going to arrange an appointment. Kathy was surprised that she hadn't noticed Emily's teeth, and she was pleased that Alice had consulted her.

"You're very welcome. We're still family," she admitted. Besides, she really liked seeing Alice there. It felt so right. "I hear you are all going shopping?" she asked, amused. Alice didn't like to shop. She liked to go in, get what she wanted without fuss, and get out. The girls' idea of shopping didn't match Alice's. "Are you taking Sean too?"

"He is welcome to come. I might need back-up…and muscles. Those girls can't lift," she confided in a conspiratorial whisper.

"I heard that," Emily put in as she brought a bowl of mashed potatoes to the table.

They all enjoyed a lively debate over the Thanksgiving dinner Kathy made, giving Mrs. Fernandez some well-deserved time off to spend with her own family. Besides, it made their housekeeper feel needed after the year of uncertainty they had all gone through in so many ways.

Sean agreed to go along for the shopping but only if he could drive. He planned on using the Rav4 to pick Alice up since the Ferrari would never hold all the purchases.

"I don't think the Rav4 can hold much more than us four passengers either," Alice pointed out, amused. She pointed to the two girls, including them in the conversation. Then, she looked at Kathy. "You want to come?"

"Oh, no. You aren't getting me involved in this. I'm going to stay home and enjoy the quiet."

Alice laughed, amused. She wasn't sure what Kathy was doing these days, and she missed that, but her wife's schedule was no longer any of her business.

They enjoyed some movies in the family movie room that night. The large screen, surround sound, and comfortable seating, was highly conducive to good movie viewing. Alice glanced at Kathy a couple times. It was not that long ago that she had confessed everything that happened to her in Russia right here in this room. She wondered if Kathy realized how much had changed in their lives since then, not all of it for the better.

"Hey, before I go," Alice said as she put on her coat to leave, "what happened when the police went through the house that last time? How did they not find the wall where I stored…" she began but lowered her voice in case any of the kids were listening. Emily had proven that they could be overheard.

"I'd used up the funds before you replaced them," Kathy pointed out. "Didn't you take your passports out?"

Alice realized she had and wondered why she hadn't thought of that. For some reason, she'd started to worry that the cops had copies of her fake passports. What the heck was wrong with her memory? She nodded

stiffly. "If you need anything..." she said as Kathy saw her out to the Ferrari.

"No, we're good. All set," Kathy told her, regretting she had ever asked her wife to leave the house and filed for divorce, but it was too late now. The divorce was well on its way to being finalized. She thought that Portia, Andi, and Alice would all be upset if she asked to halt things now. She wasn't even sure Alice wanted the divorce stopped at this point. By the new year, she should be 'free,' but Kathy knew in her heart she would never really be free. There would always be something between them, and it was not just the children they shared. "Have fun shopping tomorrow," she said with a sardonic smile, knowing Alice would hate it. Alice waved as she drove the powerful car down the driveway and out through the gate. Glancing about the nearly fully restored estate, Kathy was grateful for the fact that Alice had sent those teams around to fix the damage caused by the front-end loaders, bulldozers, and other equipment while attempting to find evidence hidden on their grounds.

* * * * *

By the first week of December, Alice's house had a new look. It was filled with the latest furniture, fixtures, and electronics. She'd had the Geek Squad in to wire the TV and its components, including a DVD player that was beyond anything she felt she wanted to tackle. The sophistication of today's electronics was something she knew she was going to have to study up on. She felt in a funk over some of it, and that pissed her off. She sat down and read through the manuals, amazed by how far a simple TV had come over the years!

She wanted to get computers again but would wait until after she swept the house for bugs. She wanted to stop by her favorite stores without the children, but they made even more trips over to her house that week as the purchases were being delivered. She didn't mind though. She enjoyed her children. Kathy got an earful about the fantastic location of her house, the stars the children were certain they had seen, and all the new items Alice had purchased. She was almost sick of hearing about it. Kit returned to college, pleased to see her mothers were adjusting to their new lives, and she soon forgot her concerns over her mothers as she got back into the routine of her own life.

Alice knew she couldn't put some things off any longer, even with the tail that followed her to Palos Verdes time and again. She managed to lose them one day, so she diverted to Beverly Hills and watched as they whizzed by the hidden driveway she pulled into. Once she was sure she had lost them, she pulled out and headed for Sebastian's home. She ended up parking two blocks away as she had been refused entry at the gate just like last time. She made her way to his neighbor's property, jumped their gate, and then made her way around the perimeter, being careful not to trip the alarm or get caught in a frame when she saw a motion-activated camera. For a long time, she had been feeling like her skills were fogged up and muddled from her inactivity. She'd gone to the house in the valley for a workout, but her car was a bit too conspicuous for that and had attracted unwelcome attention. She seriously considered selling it, angry over her impulse buy.

"Alice," Sebastian gasped, barely able to get the word out when she suddenly appeared in his bedroom. That he was still alive after such a long time must be due to his doctor's vigilance. The man should have been dead months ago—between the cancer ravaging his body and the

nurse that was killing him slowly and insidiously, gleefully taking pleasure in the pain caused by her administrations of meds. Maybe he was just imagining Alice there looking down on him like an avenging angel? "You're dead," he gasped, trying to remember if that was a dream or the truth. His hand crept to his chest where he felt his heart pounding.

"The rumors of my death have been greatly exaggerated," she told him with a grin. The smile told him that he was awake, and she was really there. "Sebastian you're alive," she stated unnecessarily, sorry to see the man so emaciated by a disease there was a cure for. Damned pharmaceutical companies and their greed!

"Is it really you?" he rasped, glancing beyond her looking for a halo, an unearthly glow, or something to indicate she had come from the beyond.

"I'm here, my friend. I'm sorry. I should have come sooner," she whispered, not wanting to bring her presence to anyone else's attention. Entering his house had been more difficult this time. They had learned from her last visit and installed more guards, monitors, and alarms. She'd had to fight against her own internal fog and really concentrate, looking for the innocent and seemingly innocuous patterns. It was the patterns that would give away the things that could catch her. She was grateful for that knowledge and vowed to train harder again. She needed to clear away her mental cobwebs.

"Kill me," she thought she heard him say. He reached out a claw-like hand, "Please?"

"You want me to kill you?" she heard herself whispering, suddenly feeling like something was clutching at her innards as she gazed upon her old friend and adversary.

"Yes, the pain of it. Nothing stops the pain, and that bitch!" he spat out the word 'bitch,' which sounded particularly nasty on his tongue, "is enjoying every moment."

"I'll take care of her for you," she promised, knowing immediately which bitch he meant.

"Will you kill me?" he pleaded.

Alice hesitated for a moment, and his eyes lowered in disappointment. "I came to visit an old friend, not to kill him," she tried to say. She was astonished to see he was still hanging on. She'd been certain her last visit would be the last time she saw him. She'd had to make certain he was gone though, as part of cleaning things up. She'd made a start, and it was important to her to methodically clean up her past, so she could begin her future, whatever it might be.

"Artum take care of your family? They safe?" he rasped out, making it hard for her to hear him despite the nearly silent room. There was one machine beeping regularly, but it was turned down low.

"No, Kathy refused his offer of help. Maybe it was all for the best?" Alice questioned honestly, seeing the flare of anger in the old man's eyes. That spark remained for just a moment before quickly fading; it required too much effort to sustain.

He sighed. He hadn't been obeyed, and Artum and his team would pay for that. He might be old and dying, but he would make sure that his orders were obeyed. Thoughts of what he would do faded as quickly as they formed. His mind was too befuddled by drugs, some prescribed by his doctor and some added for the amusement of a sadistic woman who enjoyed his pain. "Kill me?" he pleaded again, watching Alice.

"I would, Sebastian, you know I would, but it's not justified, and I've already got enough weighing on my soul. Also, you don't deserve it..." she looked at him sadly before adding a belated, "now."

"You got religion?" he started to laugh, which turned into a coughing fit.

Alice smiled widely. Her teeth were fixed now, and she was comfortable with her smile again. The idea of her going to a church, or following any organized religion, greatly amused her. "Anything else you need, my friend?" she asked, sad to see him in this condition. She glanced at the equipment setup and rose, readjusting the lines. She pulled the hose of one line from its drip, then reattached it in better order.

"Most is...taken," he said slowly, haltingly.

She waited for him to finish that sentence and then realized he had. "Pasternack?"

He nodded and said, "Some." He waited a moment, trying to gather his befuddled thoughts. "I got most of it diverted before he stole the rest. But his wife, she's something else," he added, his mind wandering again.

"Well, Sebastian, I can hear movement, and it won't be long before they discover me here. I wanted to see why you were still hanging on, you, old shyster," she teased, earning a glare from his fading eyes. She thought she saw a shadow in one of them. Perhaps it was cataracts. Still, it was obvious he could see her as his eyes followed her around the room.

"They will come," he said cryptically, but Alice didn't understand him. She frowned slightly, wondering what he meant.

"I should go before I get your people excited," she told him, touching his parchment-like hand, void of any fat below the skin. He was a skeleton.

"Avenge me," he whispered in goodbye, unable to summon the tears he wanted. He was simply too dehydrated to bother trying.

Alice looked at him once more before heading towards the door she had come through. She listened at the door momentarily before slipping out and going down the hallway to another door. She listened again and slipped through, just before footsteps on the stairs signaled someone was coming.

Artum looked down the hall and wondered where the guard outside Sebastian's bedroom had gotten to. Even the chair was missing, and that alarmed him. Slowly, he walked down the hall, listening carefully and looking through doors that were ajar, before he arrived at Sebastian's room. He cautiously opened the door, his hand on his gun, ready to pull and fire. He thought he saw something in the room and pulled his gun, leading with it as he opened the door wide, but all he found was the old man lying in his bed and looking up weakly at him.

Sebastian saw the gun coming through the door and hoped it was someone come to avenge some past crime he had committed. Instead, he was disappointed to recognize his nephew. Artum looked hale and hearty, like Sebastian had looked not too long ago, at least, that was how he saw himself in his mind. He gestured in a come-hither movement, reaching for his panic button at the same time. Before Artum even got across the room, they heard the running on the steps.

"Uncle?" he asked as he saw the button being pushed and then heard the quick steps on the stairs. Some of their men rushed into the room with guns drawn, and a few minutes later, the medical personal arrived.

Sebastian waved the medical people out, waited, and then gestured for the door to be closed. His men obeyed, although they looked at him curiously. They were glancing between Artum, who they knew was the

favored heir apparent, and the man that paid their salaries. Sebastian pointed to the now closed door and raised an eyebrow inquiringly, prompting one of the men to open it and speak to the medical personnel hovering in the hall, including Sandi Pasternack. He commanded them all to go away.

Sebastian waited, his nephew and the men waited, and finally, he closed his eyes for a moment before gesturing them all to come closer. Weakly, he asked, "What happened to Alice Weaver's family?" It was too much! Between Alice's visit and this meeting, he was exhausted. He started to cough, and it took him some time to get it under control. He peed himself, the rich aroma of urine mixing with the smells of the stale air in the sickroom.

Sebastian pointed at a window, indicating someone should open it. Gently, he sipped water from a straw as Artum helped him to sit up. He looked expectantly at his nephew. He might be old and absentminded, but he hadn't forgotten his question.

"You don't remember what I told you about that, Uncle?" Artum asked, surprised when the old man waved him to silence.

"You...told...me...nothing. Don't...lie!" he rasped, and they had to wait as another coughing fit took him. The men exchanged glances. The voice, while that of an old man, had still embodied its same commanding presence for a moment. Once he had the coughing under control, he fixed his nephew with a glare. "You will be fined for your incompetence," he managed to get out before he had to sip at the straw. The water made slurping sounds as its contents were depleted, and they waited while Artum filled the cup from the pitcher, the last of the water emptying into the cup.

"You, go and get–" began Artum, commanding one of the other men, but Sebastian waved him away.

"You…go," he countermanded, gesturing to his nephew. "Start paying penance NOW." He started to cough again, the wheezing in his chest making it hard to breathe as he hacked up phlegm and spit it into another cup. "Go!" he managed to get out before another wracking cough shook him. By now, Alice would surely have gotten away, and these incompetent fools would never know she was here. He watched as Artum took the pitcher and left the room. He fixed his eyes on the other men, unable to see them clearly but knowing their outlines. "He is to pay a penalty for disobeying my order," he got out weakly, laying back against his pillows. "Half a million," he gasped before taking a deep breath to continue and beginning to cough again. He lay there wheezing as he recovered, exhausted beyond reason. By the time Artum returned with a fresh pitcher, the condensation sending lines of moisture down the sides, Sebastian was nearly drifting off. He woke briefly to acknowledge his nephew as he filled the cup once again with cool, refreshing water. Sipping, he nodded again, thanking him without words. "Penalized…" he rasped at his nephew. "Disobeying…an…order." He waited, taking a deep breath. "Half…a…mill," he got out. He saw the brief flash of anger in Artum's eyes before he masked it and nodded, glancing at the other men. Sebastian's rheumy eyes followed the looks, and he saw only one of the men was Artum's. The others would make sure he was obeyed. He locked eyes with one of them, even if he couldn't really see the man, and the man nodded to show he would carry out Sebastian's order. He was loyal. Sebastian relaxed a little and waved them all away. He knew that he might not remember this order, but the men would. As the medical personnel returned, he saw Artum exchanging a look with the nurse,

Pasternack was the name Alice had called her. His eyes narrowed as he began to drift off, beyond exhausted at his exertions.

The medical personal made sure he was comfortable, changing his pajamas and sheets before making sure his lines were still firmly attached. Sandi had no chance to administer her own deadly concoction, despite the temptation. She had seen the look in Artum's eyes and understood the command implicitly. There were men with the medical team looking on, and she didn't dare do anything that would arouse their suspicions.

* * * * *

Alice made her way out the open bedroom window, using the lattice fastened on that side of the house. She had no idea that Artum's personal team had rushed to Sebastian's room anticipating his death. They also happened to be his bodyguards, some of his best men, but they were loyal first to Sebastian and second to Artum. This diversion had helped her avoid detection as she retraced her steps to a tree and pulled herself up with some effort, her muscles not what they once were. She climbed across to another tree, then onto a wall, keeping herself plastered against it. Finally, she made her way over the wall and into the neighbor's yard, who didn't have quite as sophisticated a security setup as Sebastian. As she jogged back to her Ferrari, she thought about how she had been expecting for months to see a notice that Sebastian had died and how he had clung tenaciously to life. She could have killed him as he asked but leaving him alive might allow him to atone for sins she wasn't even aware of. She debated about going back and giving him compassionate leave of this world but decided she really did have enough on her own shoulders.

Two cars picked up her tail on the way home. She wondered how they had found her and realized there must be a tracking device on the expensive sports car. This angered her as she had none of her tools, but that would have to change. She parked carefully, backing into the driveway and watching as the gates closed and cut off the view to her curious onlookers. She walked back to those same gates to peer out the corners and saw the two cars settle into parking spaces. Since she was dressed for jogging, she went inside and used her keyless entry to go through the house and right out the back patio onto the beach. She jogged down half a city block and used a public access path back to the PCH before she began a leisurely stroll back to her home, keeping her eye out as the never-ending traffic whizzed by. She confirmed the two cars each held two people, one a sedan and the other a souped-up Audi. She supposed whoever was watching her needed to know their car could keep up to her Ferrari if she tried to get away. But she wasn't going to try and get away; she was going to let them follow her. She turned away, returned to the public path, and headed to her patio door. As she closed it, she didn't allow herself to react when she noticed the brief flash of light that turned from red to green on her new wall-mounted TV. What the heck? She went upstairs to wash off the sweat and change her clothes when another brief flash on the new TV in her bedroom alerted her that she was being observed. Closing the bathroom door, something she hadn't felt the need to do since the kids were little, she glanced around, feeling a little paranoid.

* * * * *

The next day, Alice was up bright and early. She packed a small bag with her back to the TV, so whoever was watching couldn't see what she was packing, then she picked it up and headed out to the Ferrari, revving it twice in the still, morning air. She hoped she didn't wake any of her neighbors knowing one of them was on TV, and the other was a long-time resident without any connections to Hollywood and its fleeting fame. Slowly, she backed down the driveway, and soon, she could see the tail cars. One of them had to make an illegal U-turn on the highway to follow her down the PCH. As she drove, she admired the beautiful scenery. There was brush growing along the hills and cliffs and the ocean on the other side, much of its beach filled with houses. Occasionally, there were breaks between the houses where the city hadn't allowed anything to be built, and there it was endless sand with blue-green water as far as the eye could see. She loved the beach, but she preferred Palos Verdes. As she headed up from the beach into Santa Monica, she made sure her followers saw where she was turning as she made her way back to her old home. Once there, she let herself in, parking in front of the garage and carrying her small pack with her inside the house.

"Hello?" she called out into the silence. Wasn't anyone home? She made her way from the garage door she had effortlessly opened, wondering why Kathy hadn't changed the locks, and headed up to the house itself.

"Hello?" she called again.

"Oh, hi, Mom," Emily answered, smiling to see her there.

"Where is everybody?" she asked, disappointed that Kathy wasn't here.

"Mom took Sean to get some sneakers. His big feet keep outgrowing–" began his little sister with a touch of avarice.

"Now, now," Alice wagged her finger at her daughter, admonishing her without saying more. Sean had been very supportive of Emily when she was ill. She wouldn't let her say bad things about him, even if he teased her mercilessly sometimes. "Do you know when they will be back?"

"They just left. Want me to call?"

"No, I was hoping your mother could drive me somewhere…" she said musingly, trying to reformulate her plan.

"Something wrong with the Ferrari?" the teen asked, sounding worried.

"No, but it's too conspicuous," she said in an aggrieved tone that made her daughter laugh. Alice suddenly focused on her daughter. "Do you know how to drive?"

"I'm not old enough, remember?"

"That's not what I asked," she stated, shaking her head. Sometimes teenagers could be rather dense. "I asked if you knew how to drive?"

"Well, I went out with Mom and Sean when he was learning, of course. I've watched you and Mom for ages. I couldn't drive a stick like your Ferrari, but I know I could manage an automatic, just not on the freeway," she mused as she considered the question.

"Good. Call your friend, and you can take me over there."

"Wait! What?" she asked, alarmed. "Which friend?"

"The Pasternack chick," Alice reminded her daughter. "You are going to drive me over there. We can use the Rav4, and we'll order an Uber from there."

"Wait, I don't understand…" began Emily, confused.

"Do you want to drive the Rav4 or not?" Alice asked, making it sound like she was about to change her mind.

"Of course, I do," the girl insisted stoutly.

"Well, then, let's go. Call your friend and tell her we are coming over. You can stay until the Uber gets there and then, you can drive the car back home before your Mom gets here. Okay?"

"Mom will be so mad–" she began.

"You can tell her it was all my idea, okay?" Alice interrupted.

"Okaaay," said the teen, unconvinced.

"Let's go then. Chop! Chop!" she said, clapping her hands in time with her words. She glanced around the house as her daughter ran to change out of her pajamas, get into something more suitable, and call Carmen. Em didn't know what was going on, but she was excited.

"So, what is going on?" Emily asked as they got into the Rav4, both putting on their seatbelts. She was excited to drive the small SUV.

"I was followed over here, and I don't wish to be followed. So, you are going to help me avoid these bozos and then, when I'm gone, you can return home."

"Okay, got that." She was extremely anxious as Alice pulled the handle to lay the seat nearly flat, and when that didn't work, she put it upright again.

"Hang on," Alice ordered when the teen went to put the garage door up with the automatic clicker attached between the sun visors. Alice climbed over the console to the back seat, pulling along the small duffel bag she had brought with her. She laid down on the back seat and said, "Okay, drive."

Nervously, Em pushed the button on the garage door opener, waiting until the garage door was completely open before starting up the car. She was very conscious of her mother lying on the backseat. Checking her mirrors, she slowly put the car in gear and applied the gas. The SUV jerked as it rolled backwards into the driveway. She pressed the garage

door button again and waited for the door to close before putting the Rav4 into gear and slowly heading down the driveway. She felt exultant going down the driveway, and the sensors opened the gate as she approached when they recognized the car. As she drove through the gate, she saw the two cars that didn't belong in their neighborhood. Few, if any, of the neighbors parked on the street. Most, like her parents, had an estate with plenty of parking in the driveway. She made her way confidently over to the Pasternacks. They didn't have a security gate, and she pulled into their driveway as though she did this all the time.

Alice sat up when the SUV stopped. She had felt her daughter's anxiety and was aware when her growing confidence had replaced it. "Good job," she stated. "Call me an Uber?"

"Your phone isn't working?" the teen asked as she turned off the Rav4.

"I don't want them to trace the call to my phone," she said as she took her phone out of her pocket and slipped it under the driver's seat from the back.

"Hey, what's going on?" Carmen asked, walking up to the driver's window and frowning in surprise at her friend. She was shocked to see Mrs. Weaver sitting in the backseat, acting as though they did this every day.

"Emily is practicing her driving, and she did pretty good," Alice said dryly. She examined her daughter's friend as Emily punched in the Pasternack's address on her Uber app.

Carmen looked at Alice then back at her friend. They all knew Emily was far too young to be practicing her driving skills. She didn't even have her temps, and she hadn't taken the class offered at the high school.

"Hang on," Emily told her friend, holding up her hand. "Where to from here?" she asked her mother, but Alice grabbed the phone to enter the

address instead of replying. She was not willing to let Carmen hear the address where she was headed.

"She'll be going straight home once my ride gets here," she informed Carmen, eyeing the girl again and wondering why she didn't like her.

"Can I ride along?" Carmen asked eagerly.

"I don't think that's a good idea," Alice put in, negating the idea before they could even discuss it. Just what she needed—two girls joyriding in the neighborhood. "This was a one-time special deal for Emily," she stressed to her daughter, who got the hint right away.

Whatever was up with her mother, Emily didn't want to jeopardize it. She understood anything Alice did was to be kept under wraps. She had never told anyone what she overheard, and that had been difficult. The few times she had tried to discuss it with Kathy, she had been shut down. Alice had made it clear what her one mix-up could have cost them, and she didn't want that ever again. Keeping these secrets was costing her, but no one realized it at this point.

The Uber arrived quickly, and Alice grabbed her bag and got out. "Go right home," she warned Emily and slipped her a $20. "Later, when your mom gets home, order a pizza, and you and Carmen can share it," she said, including the neighbor girl with a smile. She waited until Emily nodded, waved goodbye to her friend, and drove off, before getting into the Uber. "Hey, thanks for the ride," she told the driver as they sped off behind Emily and the Rav4. She pretended to go through her bag at the last minute, so neither of the cars that had followed her to Palos Verdes saw her in the backseat of the SUV as they passed their location. She appreciated that the owner of the vehicle kept it very neat. She didn't speak as they drove through the streets on their way to the car rental place that she had entered in the Uber app. The Uber driver was surprised when

she paid in cash, accustomed to the app depositing payment into her account. She took it gladly, briefly wondering how she might get around paying Uber for this odd customer, then realizing she would jeopardize her standing with them if she tried that.

* * * * *

"Alice Weaver has stopped by her wife's house in Palos Verdes."

"Has she left yet? Over."

"No, she's still there. The only activity was her daughter leaving the estate, but she didn't go far, just over to one of the neighbor's houses. Now, she's just sitting there."

There was a long wait, and another car came into the area, but they didn't pay it any attention as they were watching Kathy's house for the Ferrari. Just as they reported the Rav4 returning to the Weaver estate, someone had a thought....

"The daughter isn't of driving age," came over the walkie-talkie.

The two people in the sedan exchanged glances.

"Do you think Alice Weaver was in the back of that Rav4?" one asked the other.

"That's possible," the other one replied before picking up his walkie-talkie to report. "We believe Alice Weaver may have shaken our surveillance." He wasn't happy as he explained their suspicions to the person on the other end of the mic. They had spent weeks watching her Malibu home and had done some things that weren't legal.

They were ordered to watch the Palos Verdes home in case they were mistaken, and the Ferrari eventually emerged. It was several hours later

when Kathy Weaver, not Alice Weaver, drove the Ferrari away from the estate, followed by Sean in the Rav4.

* * * * *

Alice rented a nice, little Toyota Camry. It was a sporty sedan, fast and nondescript. Driving up the 5 Freeway, she thought of the things she wanted to accomplish, and she hoped that Emily wouldn't tell Kathy too much too soon. She had things to take care of, and some of them were long overdue. Donning her first disguise at a rest stop before she got to Sacramento, she drove to her storage unit there. Once inside her unit, she jump-started the car stored there and left it running outside the unit while she talked to the owner of the facility, who happened to be manning the desk. Using the passport that matched her disguise, she closed her account. After so many years, the man was surprised, but he took her cash payment and shrugged it off. She'd been a good renter. He let her park her rental car while she took the sedan to a car wash and afterward, to a used car lot. She accepted a lot less money than she would have if it were any other car. Next, she bought a throw-away phone at a nearby store and ordered an Uber using an old email address that linked it to a bank account she rarely used. Once they dropped her at her rental car, she got in and slowly removed her disguise as she headed north.

The following day, she was in Portland doing the same thing with the Jeep she had stored there. She hated to get rid of it. Her little hidey-hole had so many uses, but this was all part of cleaning up some things. The different locks on both storage units told her that someone had been here. She suspected Kathy had figured out one location, and one could easily be

traced to the other. Now, that was history as she sold the Jeep, again for less money than she would normally have accepted.

Driving south again, she enjoyed the scenery through Mount Shasta and wished she had the time to come here camping with the children. Her version of camping would have involved an RV and a few other luxuries, which would technically make it glamping, but she wasn't about to suggest anything until she talked to Kathy and discussed the children's schedules. It had begun to rain when she arrived back in Los Angeles, but that didn't prevent her from shopping at a few of the less than reputable stores she previously frequented, some she had taken Kathy to, and a few others she hadn't been introduced to. Alice stopped at a library and used their computers to do a lot of research. She spent the day there before returning the rental car. She had an Uber take her from the rental place to her home in Malibu, only to find her Ferrari in the driveway and a party in progress. There were cars parked in her driveway and all up and down the shoulders of the PCH.

"What the hell?" she murmured as she got out of the car. The many packages in her arms suddenly felt heavy as she observed the teenagers coming and going in her courtyard. They were acting as though they owned the house and property and looking at her curiously. Pushing past some, she stopped in the garage to put down her bags and continued into her house, looking for someone she recognized.

"Mom?" Sean asked when he saw his mother. He was surprised to see her. He had thought she would be gone all weekend. Kathy had brought the Ferrari home, and Sean and his friends had come over, ostensibly to use the beach and play video games. Someone had arrived with alcohol, and things were rapidly getting out of hand as word spread and more and more people came.

"Are you kidding me?" Alice asked him, remembering the party in Palos Verdes where she had been forced to throw several kids out.

"Mom, I just invited–"

"I don't care who you invited. Get them out of *my* home NOW!" The last word of that command came out in a roar as Alice went to a closet and removed a baseball bat, hefting it as she approached the TV in the living room. Some of the kids were watching videos on the seventy-two-inch screen Sean had talked her into buying, and others were dancing, the surround sound blasting in the beachside home. She had seen the red light on the TV quickly switch to green then turn off completely, and without hesitation, she began to smash the large-screen television.

"MOM!" Sean yelled, aghast. He turned to the friends he knew, shouting, "Get out! GET OUT NOW!" There was a mad exodus as Alice finished smashing that large-screen TV and began to push the mass of teenagers out of her way as she headed towards the stairs, beginning to work her way upstairs. "Mom NO!" Sean called, trying to follow her, but the press of bodies was hard to fight against, and she had already smashed the TV in his room, the TV in Em's room, and was advancing on her own room when he reached her. She smashed her TV too, stomping on it as it fell to the floor and ripping out the wires behind it. "Why, Mom?" he asked, feeling heartbroken at the devastation he had witnessed. He held his head and tears began to streak down his young face. He could hear the last of the guests encouraging others to get out of the house.

Alice looked up at her son. She was forced to look up because he was so much taller than she. Her heart wrenched seeing his tears. She glanced at the computer games that his friends had been playing on the big-screen TV she installed in his room, which now lay in tatters. She pulled his hands down and shook her head. He stared at her incredulously. Putting a

finger to her lips, she gestured that they should go downstairs. Sean was hesitant at first, then curious, and he followed her. She led him to the garage where she had put several heavy bags and pulled out a couple gadgets. She soon had them working after inserting batteries, and using them, she found four bugs in her garage alone.

"What...?" he began but she put her finger to her lips again and shook her head to silence him.

She demonstrated how the gadget worked, and she showed him the bugs she'd found, again putting her finger to her lips. She mouthed, *"We are being monitored."* Staring wide-eyed, Sean nodded. Over the next two hours, they pulled dozens of innocuous-looking plaster plugs from her walls, putting the bugs they found beneath them all in baggies and placing them in the freezer.

Alice and Sean went over the house twice. Sean had used the weaker of the two devices she purchased, and she went over it one last time with her own hand-held monitor that was able to sense the electronics from these devices. She went over the smashed TVs, unhooking them from their wires but not before zooming in on the electronic eyes that had been installed in the new TVs. Equipped with internet streaming and facial recognition capabilities, they had made her vulnerable to intrusion by whoever was monitoring her.

"What the hell was that all about?" Sean finally asked after hours of silence while they pulled the bugs that were cleverly hidden beneath the plaster in her walls and inside the TVs. His heart wept over the loss of the huge TVs. He had thought Alice was just pissed off over the party, and he had never seen her that angry before.

"These next-generation smart TVs and devices run some pretty sophisticated software. With my internet connection and the integrated

sensors," she indicated those she had pulled from the TVs to examine, "like these microphones, they can watch whoever is in the house. I noticed last week that the red signal, which I hadn't turned on, was coming on seemingly at will and turning green sporadically, and I realized someone was watching me through the TVs."

"Even when you were alone or getting dressed? What about in my room?" he asked, outraged.

"Possibly. What'd you do that I might not want to know about?" she asked.

"I changed my clothes…" he began, suddenly realizing the implications of this spyware as he surveyed all the equipment Alice had shown him. "What else can they do?" he asked in an attempt to change the subject. He didn't want Alice to know about the girlfriend he had in here before the party began. They'd taken the Ferrari out for a spin as well as some other things he didn't think any mother should know about.

"They can change channels, adjust the volume, cyberstalk us, and record us."

He stared at the electronics, horrified and wondering if he was about to be blackmailed by some unknown watcher. "How long–?" he began, remembering how excited he had been to get these things and now, they were smashed, and Alice was cleaning up the mess.

"Help me clean this up," she indicated the electronics and glass on the floor. She'd sent the message she intended. Whoever had bypassed the manufacturer or Geek Squad's install had gotten more than they intended on their end. The bonus was, she had frightened Sean's friends, and they wouldn't be partying at her home again anytime soon. "We can discuss your punishment for driving my Ferrari."

"How did you–?" he began, but she interrupted him and placed a damaged TV by the door.

"You just told me," she answered dryly, shaking her head at how easy it was to fool her son.

They brought the three TVs down from upstairs and placed them up against the first one. Alice had Sean vacuum up the glass and small plastic pieces from both floors as she installed new security features, things that only she would touch during installation. It was quite late when a phone on the counter rang. Alice realized it was her own cell phone and answered it.

"Is Sean with you?" Kathy asked as soon as Alice said hello.

"Yes, he's cleaning his room as punishment," she said dryly.

"Punishment?"

"For the party I walked in on when I got home this afternoon. Thanks for putting the Ferrari in the driveway and bringing my phone back."

"What the heck was up with that? Why did–?"

"We have to talk about that in person, you know what I mean?" she cautioned, certain that her phone was bugged, or she was still being listened to by some other method. She decided it was about time she figured out who *they* were.

Kathy sighed. She had been hoping that with the divorce they would be done with such things, but she had to admit she'd enjoyed driving Alice's Ferrari. It was a hot, little sports car, but she hadn't imagined that Sean would go back to party when he followed her and gave her a ride home. She needed to talk to Alice about having Uber pick her up here at the house, and she didn't know that Emily had driven the Rav4 yet. "I guess I'll talk to you about it tomorrow when you drop Sean off?"

"I'll do that," she promised, wondering if Kathy really wanted to know. She went back to opening her many packages.

"A new computer?" Sean asked when he finished vacuuming. There had been a lot of small glass shards but only because Alice had hit the TVs so violently and so many times. He'd vacuumed thoroughly, running the vacuum one way and then the other in all the rooms, and he had emptied the cannister in the garbage several times. He knew a shoddy job would earn his mother's ire, and right now, he was certain he didn't want to face that again.

"A network," she corrected, pulling another laptop from the bag. "I need to get a desktop too."

"Setting up your old system?" he asked. He had always admired the system on her desks in the old house. He hadn't understood it, and he had been too young to touch it, but it always looked impressive.

"Yeah, I thought I should get back into investing. It will give me something to do and keep my days busy." Also, she needed to do research. Only certain programs would do that for her, and she needed dedicated systems for that. But she didn't share that information with her son; he didn't need to know.

"Can I come with you when you get the desktop?"

Alice glanced up at her tall, sturdy son. "I was thinking about asking your mom to go with me, so we could discuss your punishment for this unplanned party and driving my car without permission."

"I thought cleaning up the mess was–?"

"You thought cleaning up was your full punishment? C'mon, Sean. You really thought you would get off that easy?" She fixed him with a look that had him squirming slightly.

"I guess not," he answered lamely, looking down to get away from her penetrating stare and shuffling his feet uncomfortably. "Do you realize how many of my friends are going to tell people you're mental after that little display," he gestured to the four TV corpses leaning against the wall near the front door.

"Good! Then they won't mess with me, especially when I'm swinging a bat," she smiled to show she was teasing and saw him grin ruefully. He knew she loved him, but the display of temper he had seen had been impressive. He didn't care what people thought of his mom. He was just grateful she was back in their lives. "How about I replace the TVs, and you help me program the new ones, so no one can do that again?" she gestured to the pile of electronics she had pulled from the TVs that was all garbage now.

"You're going to buy new TVs?" he asked, surprised. He liked that idea. It had been fun buying the first new ones and seeing the latest technology.

"Yeah, but if they need to backorder any of them, I'm not buying them. Either they give me what is on hand in their warehouse, or I'm passing."

He thought about it for a second before nodding. "We'll need Mom's car or the Rav4," he warned her.

"That's why I thought I'd ask your mom to come. Maybe I should get a more practical SUV?" she wondered aloud, looking up from the two laptops she was setting up. One laptop was already set to go, and she could use the router to hook it up to the internet. She wanted an intranet in the house too, one that intruders couldn't get into. She also had a few programs to install but would wait until Sean wasn't around.

"You'd buy another car?" he asked eagerly, hoping to get one for himself eventually. He'd hinted many times, but his mothers had ignored

him. He knew they could afford it, but he wasn't going to push, especially now, while punishment was on the table.

"Yeah, I'm thinking the Ferrari is fun but too impractical. I love your mom's Lexus, but again, that's a sports car and not roomy enough to haul things," she said as she considered her options and supplied information when the screen requested it. "You better get some sleep. We'll take you home tomorrow," she told him.

"Okay. Good night, Mom," he said, giving her a kiss on the cheek, so he could get a glimpse at the two screens of her laptop. One was still loading things.

Alice knew her children well, which was why she hadn't pulled out programs they were better off not knowing about. Hell, she hadn't even bought some of them yet.

* * * * *

"What the hell is going on?" Kathy asked as they drove the Rav4 instead of her much-preferred Lexus. Alice had explained there simply wasn't enough room in the Lexus for what she wanted to purchase. They'd decided not to take Sean as they needed to talk in private.

"I honestly don't know yet, but I'm taking steps to find out," Alice responded, telling her wife what she had found in the plaster of the walls and in the TVs. She was going to have to stop at the hardware store for supplies to repair the damage of the various holes in her walls. It had been a slick job, and she wanted to keep going over the whole place but knew her obsessive behavior wouldn't net anything more.

They went to the house in Malibu and loaded up the damaged TVs, tying the seventy-two-inchers to the top of the Rav4 since they wouldn't fit

inside, then taking them all to the dump. She was unhappy to learn she had to pay an electronics fee to dispose of them.

"What did you do to those?" Kathy asked, and Alice described the performance she had put on for the sake of the teenagers who were partying at her house. She'd already fielded several phone calls from concerned parents and quickly made her point that the kids shouldn't have been partying unsupervised in her house without permission. By asking if it was their child that brought the liquor, Alice had quickly ended several of those angry phone calls. Knowing Alice, Kathy was quite certain that the tales weren't overly exaggerated, and she was certain that being unapologetic would serve them well against these parents.

"So, are the listening devices anything like the ones Linda planted?"

"No, these are much more sophisticated. They put them in the nail holes of the plaster, so they looked like they belonged there. I didn't notice because they probably used quick-drying cement and then painted. I have no idea when they did all that, and we just bought the TVs, so I don't even know if it's the same people that bugged them or if it's the government."

"But you are immune from prosecution!" Kathy said, naively.

"For past deeds, not future ones," Alice pointed out.

"What about me and the kids? Are we safe?"

Alice quickly waved around the device she had brought along to use in the car, then she and Kathy headed off to get rid of the TVs and buy a new desktop computer, several monitors, and four new televisions. The store tried to arrange for delivery when the seventy-two-inch TVs didn't fit in the car, but Alice refused delivery. She also declined to purchase the first two TVs she had chosen, which were out of stock. She wouldn't buy anything that wasn't readily available. With Christmas approaching, the

stores were really limited as to what stock they had on hand, unless she wanted to wait. Alice wouldn't wait, preferring to be thought of as a difficult customer. They drove away with a full load, choosing alternate TVs and strapping one to the top of the car, although the store didn't recommend laying it flat.

"Careful," Kathy winced as they went over one those infernal dips on the sides of each road and water splashed up the sides of the car. It had stopped raining, and Alice was anxious to get this load to her house and start installing it by herself. That was the only way she could be certain that no other additions were made to her new purchases.

"I just don't want to be caught in the rain with that strapped to the roof," Alice said, pointing to the box she could just barely see through the sunroof. She was certain it wasn't good for the nice TV to be lying on its back, but she hoped the styrofoam they used to pack those things would keep it from getting damaged. The store staff had repeatedly tried to convince her to allow them to deliver it. She'd bought a lot from them the past few days, so they were eager to please, but she expressed her impatience and insisted she didn't want to wait. What she really didn't want was to give someone an opportunity to install more surveillance equipment. Already, her phone had picked up someone looking around the outside the house a bit too long for her comfort. The new equipment she had methodically installed was already working, sending her notifications over the program she had installed on her phone and Bluetoothing the information there.

"Is it the government?" Kathy murmured, surveying the wet hillsides that had been inundated by El Nino and the storms it generated.

"Probably, but I think there is more at work here than just that. I must start doing my homework," Alice answered. She glanced at Kathy as she

drove, wondering why she was pursuing this divorce. They still got along well, and the anger had passed. Here she was helping Alice decorate her new home in Malibu.

Kathy started to ask if Alice needed any help but swallowed the words before they emerged, not wanting to get involved. She had to learn to turn that off. After all their years together, it was second nature, and she really did want to help Alice, but she had to learn to stop. That wasn't going to be easy.

Kathy helped Alice carry her boxes into the house. They took the TVs out of the large boxes one by one and hung them up. Alice could wire them herself but hanging them was tough because they were too unwieldy.

"How do you know they won't bug these too?" Kathy asked.

"I already looked it up. Smart TVs have security settings. You can change the default network passwords that the manufacturer set up." She gestured with the channel changer she was inserting batteries into. "There is also a way to disable the microphones and cameras. If that doesn't work, this should," she said as she took some electrical tape and covered the camera on the seventy-two-inch TV. They shared a grin. It was barely noticeable on the TV and such a simple fix.

Kathy left while Alice was installing software updates on her new TVs. She never saw when Alice hauled the boxes for her new monitors and computer into her office to set them up, completely forgetting that she didn't even have a desk yet. She sighed. Asking Kathy to help her again went against her grain, so she looked online with the laptop to find what she wanted and arranged next-day delivery. She spent her time constructively. The TVs were the simplest to set up, followed by the computers and the programs she needed to install. They were nothing that normal people would use, but they were things that someone in Alice's

line of work required. She began her research over the next few days, allowing only one interruption by the desk delivery people. Once the desk was set up, she placed her new computers on it strategically, so she could still enjoy the view of the expensive real estate she had purchased with her new beach home.

* * * * *

During her research, Alice read that Sebastian had died. Saddened, she read the obituary closely again and realized she could still attend the funeral if she stopped what she was doing immediately and changed. While setting up the computers, she had made changes to the programming and customized the setup, so it worked only for her. The dummy laptop would be a little easier to use for the unknowing. It was a good fake out should anyone with any knowledge of encrypted software try to get on. She had known it was just a matter of time before her old computers would eventually be broken into, but in these computers, the software, and even the hardware, was so much more sophisticated.

Driving the Ferrari with her tails following, she was annoyed enough that she decided to make it difficult for them to tag along. As she made her way to the funeral home, she maneuvered through traffic as though people and their cars were merely a minor inconvenience, the powerful engine easily powering up as she applied pressure to the gas pedal. Arriving at the funeral home, she realized she had a reprieve from them for maybe a few minutes. She saw several of Sebastian's men including Artum, his nephew. One she especially remembered was looking just like the hood she remembered. Wearing black sweats to a funeral was a stereotype, if ever she saw one. He was pathetic when he tried to look

menacing with his thick gold chains hanging down the front V of his track suit.

"Artum," Alice said kindly, her expensive suit showing off her new, slimmer figure. Alice had gotten a haircut, and her spikes were something she enjoyed now with her hair shaped into an elegant style.

"Alice," he responded, leaning down to shake her hand and bestow a kiss on her cheek. She smelled of some heavenly perfume.

"I am sorry for your loss. He was quite a man," she stated as she glanced beyond the line of men accepting condolences, most of whom she did not know and who were obviously there as a show of strength behind Artum.

Artum looked from the petite blonde to his uncle's casket and nodded. His uncle had cost him half a million dollars in penance for not guarding this woman's family properly. He already knew the money had been placed out of his reach, but he didn't know where. Pasternack was searching but hadn't found it yet. He glanced at his men, noting the attention a few of them were paying the older woman. He wondered if any of them had heard the stories his uncle told him. He didn't know if he quite believed them, but it didn't pay to totally ignore what his uncle said. He had a lot of work to do in the coming weeks as he secured his place in this world, especially now that he had his hands on his uncle's holdings. He appreciated that Alice had come to pay her respects, that spoke well of her. He glanced around at the others attending the viewing, some out of fear and others out of genuine respect.

Alice glanced around the room, not intending to stay for the service. As she started to make her way through the throng of well-wishers, she spotted the Pasternacks waiting in the line that had formed. She didn't know why, but they grated on her nerves. Richard nodded cordially,

recognizing her as their former neighbor. He had planned to purchase their estate when it went into foreclosure with the IRS, but that had somehow been thwarted, and he wondered how and why. She recognized Sandi on a basic level that they both apparently recognized. Sandi stared at Alice coldly, and then, much to their mutual chagrin, she smiled. Alice returned her smile ever so slightly, realizing it was a feral challenge of some sort.

* * * * *

"Find it," he ordered the banker, wondering where the rest of his uncle's money had gone. Some of it seemed to have vanished into thin air, and he needed funds to enact the changes he wanted to see in the organization he had inherited. Dismissing the banker, he turned to his men and called them in individually, so they could report on their own small pieces of the pie and the monies they were earning for his organization.

"You aren't producing, Ignat," he said formally, knowing the man hated his full and proper name and preferred to be called 'Iggy.' "You either start bringing me more or your failures will be called into account," he indicated the accounting books he had been going over.

Iggy shifted. He was uncomfortable in the track suit he was wearing today. It concealed some of his bulk, but most of it was fat because he was essentially lazy. "I produce," he protested, taking it personally since he had also been called on the carpet for dressing inappropriately at the funeral. He had thought the track suit in black was suitable, and it was brand new. Apparently, these Americans wanted him to wear suits, but he hated how constricting a tie felt.

"Are you arguing with me, Ignat?" Artum asked menacingly, no longer the associate under the thumb of his uncle but very much in command.

"No. Sir," he added belatedly, realizing that Artum could order his death with very little effort.

"Good, then there is hope you are listening," the man said derisively. "You better find some merchandise to bring in soon. You have two weeks."

"Only two?" he began to whine but stopped himself. At the same instant he realized it was Christmas and people would have a lot of new gadgets that he and his men could steal. "Yes, sir. Two weeks," he corrected himself before Artum could chastise him for his tone. "I'll have it."

"Good," Artum said dismissively, never seeing the resentment burning in the eyes of his subordinate.

* * * * *

"Hello?" Alice answered her phone, surprised that Kathy had called. She'd been so involved in her research and new computer setup that she had barely eaten, much less communicated with anyone in the past few days. She'd only stopped to go to Sebastian's funeral. That had been a well-needed break, and she was grateful because it gave her footage of those trying to get into her house while she was gone. She was now looking into who these people were and hoping to trace them back to their employers. Photo imaging software was so much better than it had been just a few years ago. Her scanner, the camera shots, and a few clicks of the button, sent them searching through massive databases. Already, she had identified four of her followers and was now tracing their employers.

She was also finding out who owned the cars and hacking into one of those two employers' networks. Hacking the networks without a trace was the key because it gave her so much more information than she needed.

"We never decided what Sean's punishment should be regarding the party and driving the Ferrari?" Kathy began, feeling nervous about asking Alice to Christmas. It really wasn't something she wanted to do, but the kids deserved a normal holiday for a change and excluding Alice wouldn't solve anything.

"I was thinking about that," Alice told her. She had done nothing of the kind, but she didn't feel she had to tell Kathy the whole truth anymore. "We should tell him the truck we were going to buy him for Christmas was returned, and he won't get one until graduation IF he keeps up his grades."

"Oh, that's diabolical," Kathy admired. Then in almost the same breath she asked, "You didn't buy him one, did you?"

"No, did you?" Alice asked, suddenly amused.

"No, but were you going to?"

"I hadn't really thought of it, although I didn't miss one of his hints. Now, if he thinks he blew it, he'll probably keep himself in line until graduation next year."

"Good point," Kathy laughed. She had wanted to buy him a truck, something he would have really liked showing off to his football buddies and his other geeky friends. It would really devastate him to learn that he lost it. "Should I tell him, or would you like the honors?"

"Maybe we shouldn't be this mean," Alice reconsidered. She'd said it on impulse and perhaps it was too harsh.

"Tell you what, go pick up one of those Hot Wheel trucks, and we'll give him that. We'll tell him that we decided not to give him the real thing

because of his irresponsibility, but if he keeps his nose clean between now and graduation, he will get the real thing."

"And when should we do this?" Alice asked, amused.

"Well, I was calling to invite you to Christmas. I think the kids should have as normal a holiday as possible, and I want to have it here," she answered, holding her breath to hear what Alice thought.

"Okaaay," she drawled out, wondering at this.

"But we can punish Sean as soon as you want. Why don't you come to dinner tonight, and we'll tell him then?"

"Something to look forward to," Alice murmured into the phone quietly.

"What was that?" Kathy asked, not quite hearing her.

"Do you want me to bring anything besides the toy truck?" Alice asked, louder this time.

"Nope, I have the fixings for a roast. I'll put that in, and you can be here by five?"

"Sounds good," Alice said as she rang off, wondering if they were being too harsh on Sean. She'd already heard from Emily that people at school had been talking about her and calling her mental for her reaction to a *little* party. Emily had gotten into trouble at school for loudly defending her mother over the incident.

Alice finished up her work and showered, looking at her hair and deciding she needed more mousse for this style. She really liked the spikey look these days. The sun here at the beach, on the days it wasn't rainy from the winter storms, were bleaching her hair a pleasant shade of blonde.

Stopping at a store she knew would carry toy cars and trucks, she found the one her son wanted—a red Chevrolet Avalanche. She wrapped it up

and brought it with her to the Palos Verdes estate. She missed living here. The quiet and the space made it feel like home. She felt much more comfortable there since she'd had years to make it their own. She didn't have that in Malibu, but she accepted her circumstances. She would make it her home…eventually. Things were what they were. She slipped the wrapped package to Kathy, who put it on Sean's plate before dinner.

"Did you get me this?" he asked excitedly as he opened the package and saw it was an exact replica of the vehicle he wanted.

"No, Sean. That's what you lost this Christmas," Alice told him, looking him straight in the eye and waiting for him to look away from her direct gaze.

"We decided that the truck Momma A bought you for Christmas had to go back," Kathy told him, using the moniker the kids had assigned to Alice. "You're too irresponsible to handle one of your own yet." Kathy always tried to present a united front to their children.

Emily's mouth gaped open as she watched her moms punish her brother.

"But—" he began to argue.

"Just be glad I didn't sue any of those children's parents for trespassing," Alice warned. "California has some interesting laws," she added, as though just making conversation with her family.

"If you keep your grades up and don't screw up like this again, we'll revisit the idea of your own vehicle when you graduate high school," Kathy told him, and he looked up at her, furious.

"That's a year and a half away! It was only a party, for Christ's sake!"

"You watch your mouth when you're speaking to your mother!" Alice roared, standing up. Kathy put her hand on Alice's arm to calm her, knowing she would take their son on physically, if she had to.

Sean stared defiantly at both his parents before looking down at his plate and seeing the reminder of his mistake sitting there in its plastic container. He'd wanted an Avalanche for a while now, had really been hoping for it, but he would have settled for a sports car. "It's not like we can't afford–" he began, using arguments he had heard from his friends.

"Really? You have an abundance of cash?" Alice asked him, still standing and looking at the fine young man that was her son. She was wondering if his defiance was going to continue.

"We have trust funds…" he began, looking up.

"You've been listening to the wrong people," Kathy put in, suddenly sounding angry. "You do not have any money. You *don't* work. You go to school, and your allowance is all the money you have."

"It's not like you can't afford–" he began again, hotly.

"Neither can you," Alice finished for him, her voice sarcastic.

He looked up at the tone and realized that defying his moms wouldn't get him the truck he coveted. The fact that they said they might discuss a vehicle when he graduated did give him hope. "How am I supposed to get to my football practice and–"

"How have you been getting there now?" Alice asked as she sat down. Kathy's hand released her arm as she fussed with a napkin to cover her embarrassment over having touched her wife.

"The bus and friends," he answered, sounding sullen.

"Then you will continue to do that, and make sure you aren't a piker—contribute to their gas tanks."

He was angry and started to get up.

"Where are you going?" Alice asked him. "Your mother made a delicious dinner, and even if you don't eat it, you'll sit here while we enjoy it." Something in her tone told him not to leave the table. He wasn't

afraid of Alice, but he had seen her whip that one football player's butt, and the smashing of those TVs was still fresh in his mind. Maybe his friends were right? Maybe Alice was mental?

Dinner was rather tense, but Alice ignored the tension as she enjoyed the food Kathy had prepared for her. Kathy insisted she stay for dessert, a sullen Sean eating only half the food he normally inhaled. His metabolism as a growing young man and football player burned off almost all he ate as soon as he put it into his system.

"Can we play some family games?" Emily asked hopefully after dinner when they had all chipped in to clean the table and get the dishes into the dishwasher.

"May I go to my room?" Sean asked politely, and his mothers took pity on him. Alice made sure he took the model of the Avalanche with him as he stomped up the stairs to his room. Kathy went to the control panel and turned off the internet and cable for Sean's room. They both heard his protests, but then it got quiet.

"He's rather hurt," she whispered to Kathy as Emily went to get a board game called Stratego that they played occasionally. It was a game for two players and required deep concentration as they were warring with each other.

"He thought he got off scot-free, and I resent that," Kathy whispered back, handing Alice some ice water as she would be driving later, feeling it was better than any of the wines they would have normally indulged in.

"He learned different," Alice answered, taking a drink and hearing Emily return.

"He sure did," Kathy murmured in reply, her voice low enough that their daughter didn't hear. She took an unnecessary swipe at the counter to

finish cleaning up before hanging the rag over the edge of the sink to dry out.

Alice played against Emily first, then Emily played Kathy before the two moms challenged each other. Emily went to bed. It took a long time for the competition to complete, but Alice won in the end. She smiled at Kathy as she took her wife's flag. Not one to gloat, she smiled and stretched, showing off her body against her shirt. Kathy turned away, feeling a sudden bolt of desire shoot through her as she began to clean up the game pieces.

They put away the game, and Alice readied herself to go out in the lashing rain.

"Damn, it's coming down. Let me get an umbrella," Kathy offered.

"It's cold too. You don't have to come out with me," Alice told her as she put on her coat. It *was* cold, and she could see that fog had rolled in a bit. Her breath condensed to steam as she stepped out onto the small porch and peered into the darkness.

"Nonsense," Kathy objected, pulling on her own jacket and holding up the umbrella she had grabbed. She walked Alice down to the expensive sports car. The rain was splashing onto the asphalt and concrete and bouncing up at her, wetting her jeans from the knees down as she held up the umbrella while Alice got in the low-slung vehicle. She wished Alice didn't have to go but stoically kept her silence.

"Thank you," Alice said, puzzled by the look she thought she saw in Kathy's eyes. It must be a trick of the lights. They had always called them the landing lights because they showed the walkway but were not too bright on the rain-swept path.

"Drive safely," Kathy said as Alice backed away. She was tempted to lean in for a kiss goodbye but knew it was inappropriate now and would

only confuse the situation. "Thanks for coming!" she called as she waved. Alice waved back, closed the door, and started the car. Kathy hurried up the steps, aware that Alice watched her before turning the car around and driving down the long drive. The hum of the engine sounded more like the purr of a cat. *Appropriate for someone like Alice*, Kathy thought.

Alice almost felt sorry for the two sedans waiting for her. They couldn't help but see her headlights, which alerted them to the fact that she was leaving. She fishtailed slightly, showing off as she sped past them, the powerful engine easily eating up the paved road and roaring away from them. They both hurriedly started their engines and sped after their quarry. Their orders were to watch her and follow her, and since she now knew of their presence, they also tried to annoy her. They all judiciously ignored each other.

They did annoy Alice. That was probably why she chose to take the longer way home that night…it wasn't the fact that she wished she was going back to the house in Palos Verdes, and it wasn't the fact that she desperately wanted to be taking a hot bath with Kathy and later, twining her limbs around her soon-to-be ex-wife. According to the paperwork, they would both be free by the new year. Driving onto the PCH, she was lost in thought as she expertly outdistanced her pursuers. The powerful engine continued to eat up the pavement as she applied a little more pressure to the gas pedal. Only the fact that the traffic lights slowed her gave them any hope of catching up. Occasionally, she slipped through a yellow light in time to lose them for a bit longer. She could have turned off, but they all knew she was headed to her other home.

Peering through the downpour, she slowed a bit. The puddles were becoming a bit deep for her almost brand-new car, and the ditches were running full. Anyone foolish enough to be out walking in this was sure to

by swamped by any car passing them on the road. In fact, she saw more than one person enjoying the ditches and deliberately spraying water on the poor, wretched individuals who were unfortunate enough to be waiting at bus stops and huddling under the overhangs to avoid the downpour. She didn't find it funny, and in her mood, she was tempted to run one of them off the road. She constrained herself as her mood worsened.

As she was driving along with the headlights behind her rushing to catch up, she glanced behind her. The distinctive shape of one sedan's headlights told her he was catching up. She glanced forward just in time to hit the brake sharply as a boulder crashed down in front of her, bounced once, and rolled across the highway. She pulled around it just in time to get out of the way of a second boulder, but just when she thought she had passed the cliffs that were eroding from the rain, an entire chunk of hillside crashed down on the PCH. Alice wasn't as fortunate this time. One boulder bounced onto the hood of her car, spinning her, and the next one crashed over the roof and into the passenger side door. The window shattered, making a horrific sound, and she spun even farther. Alice was trying to control the car but was unable to turn out of the path of the oncoming mud, gravel, and boulders. Another one bounced over the car and hit the edge of the driver's side door, bending the frame. The open passenger window allowed rain-soaked dirt and gravel to spill onto the leather seat, rapidly filling that side of the car. The engine sputtered to a halt, trapping her and preventing her from moving out of the path of the oncoming deluge. She could hear the scrapes as the rocks, boulders, and gravel all hit her car.

Alice pushed against the driver's side door, watching in consternation as the passenger side of the vehicle continued to fill rapidly. She couldn't open her door; the bent frame was preventing that. The back windshield

exploded from the force of the debris building up on top of the car. She tried to use her elbow to break the window but only hurt herself instead. Alice grabbed the headrest on the passenger side, trying to yank it out and failing. The dirt and rocks were too high, and they were still coming. She could hear the metal over her head beginning to groan in protest at the additional weight. She pulled at her own headrest, yanking and jerking and pushing the adjustment button that held it in place until it finally pulled free. She looked at the two metal prongs, then she pulled back and hit her driver's side window with them. They were designed to break the glass. The first blow didn't do anything but hurt her hand, and with her elbow already smarting, she didn't appreciate the added pain. She was desperate and trying not to panic. She kept hitting the window with the headrest, the soft leather protecting her hand from cuts, and the window finally splintered when one of the prongs penetrated it. She kept bashing at the window until she thought there was enough room for her to climb out. She dropped the headrest and tried to get out, but her seatbelt held her back. She heard the top of her car collapsing, the metal grinding even lower, and she saw her open window start to settle. The glass was no longer helping the metal support the roof and prevent it from caving in. She jabbed at her seatbelt release, finally feeling it give. As she pulled herself up again and tried to get through the window, she realized that the crushed engine had her right leg trapped below the dash. She tugged, but it wouldn't give. Her upper body was partly out the window, and the shards of glass were digging into her coat and ripping it to shreds as she struggled to pull her leg free. The rain was coming down, nearly drowning her. Then, she realized it wasn't rain. Dirt and debris were still coming down with the rockslide and pouring across the roof of her car. The

ensuing mud was drowning her. The groaning of the metal was horrendous as her vehicle succumbed to the weight and slowly buckled.

Alice pulled and yanked at her leg; her back was being cut as it rubbed against the jagged edges of the broken window. As the hood settled once more under the weight of the onslaught, she realized she could no longer feel her leg, and she began to see spots through the mud and debris as she rapidly blinked it away through the rain. She could hear the pulse pounding in her ears, replacing the roar of the landslide and the scrape of stone against metal. Everything went black.

~The End~ K'Anne ;-

If you have enjoyed **METHODICAL MALICE,** I hope you will
enjoy this excerpt from

FLIGHT

A tragic explosion results in the death of over 200 airplane passengers. Was the explosion caused by pilot error, or was it a conspiracy?

Pilot Cathalene (Lena) Penn, accused by the airline of being a smuggler, died in the tragedy, and her wife, Jessica is desperate to clear Lena's good name.

When Jessica travels to Belgium, her wife's home away from home, she discovers diamonds, a second family, and a mystery...

Sometimes, choosing between what is safe and what is right isn't easy, and running away is always an option...Flight!

CHAPTER ONE

Bam! Bam! Bam! The banging woke Jessica from a sound sleep. At first, she blinked, thinking she had dreamt the noise. Then, it was repeated a second and a third time. Her heart began thumping in fear when she realized she wasn't dreaming, and the noise that had woken her was someone beating a tattoo on her front door. Her first instinct was to get up, run, and hide, but then logical thought took over. Slowly, she rose from the bed, grasping for her robe lying at the end. She covered her nakedness, but before she had the robe completely on, she heard the incessant beating on the front door start up once again. If whoever that was left marks on her lovely wood door, she'd give them an earful. Jessica glanced at the clock, noting it read 3:10 a.m. She glanced out the window at the solid darkness of the early morning. Sighing, she reached for the handle of the bedroom door and heard the tattooing on the front door erupt once again. Gawd, someone was

persistent. She flipped on the hall light as she went out, and the pounding, which had been coming in spates of three, immediately stopped between the second and third knock. Slowly, she squinted into the dark, trying to see who was there. She knew for sure an intruder wouldn't knock so persistently. Jessica headed cautiously down the curving staircase towards the front door.

Making sure the chain was latched, she turned on the outside light in order to see better. Slowly, she unlocked the door, in no hurry as she saw a man in a coat, a suit visible beneath its unbuttoned opening. Her heart was beating as hard as he had been pounding on the door, a static tattoo with missed beats that she knew didn't signal anything good. She wasn't sure the beats weren't a precursor of a tearing wrench that was about to come.

"Hello?" she asked when she got the door ajar.

"Mrs. Penn?" he asked, peering at her through the door. The light from the porch barely lit her face and everything behind her was in darkness.

Seeing the captain's wings on his collar, she realized what this visit must mean and asked simply, "When?"

"May I come in, Mrs. Penn?" he asked, ignoring her question.

Gulping, she nodded and closed the door to remove the chain. She pulled the door open slightly, turned away, and walked a few paces to the newel post on the stairs. Her back was to her guest, who let himself in. She asked again, "When?"

"One a.m. local time," he answered, knowing she had guessed the reason for his visit.

Jess' hand spasmodically squeezed the post in response. Clutching it slightly for its stability, she took a deep breath before releasing both the post and the breath and heading down the hall along the stairs. She could hear by the steps behind her that the man was following her. She went through the swinging door to the kitchen, flipping the switch to turn on the light. Sitting at the breakfast bar, she stared numbly, seeing nothing as she waited. She was superficially aware as the man rummaged in her cupboards for a cup and poured her some water from the tap.

"Here, drink this," he offered kindly, watching her face closely.

She took the cup and drank from it, not aware that she was thirsty, or the liquid in the cup was merely water. "Were there any survivors?" She was grasping at straws, any hope, maybe they were just bracing her for the reality of the damage.

He shook his head. He waited. They were both quiet a long time, then a slight noise from upstairs made them both jump. He glanced up, but Jess didn't budge.

"She'll go back to bed," she stated to no one in particular. In fact, they heard the squeak of the floorboards once more a few minutes later before silence overcame the house once again. Finally, Jess looked up at the man, gazing in surprise to find him there as memories had assailed her. "Who are you?" she finally asked.

"I'm with the union. I'm here…to help," he explained, feeling helpless. The devastation written on her face was worse than he had expected, although he hadn't really known quite what to expect.

"Are they finding…" she gulped before continuing, "any bodies?"

"They are already on the scene investigating and looking for anything."

She glanced at him sharply. "There are no survivors?"

He shook his head, denying her that last false hope.

She took a deep breath, letting it out slowly and wanting it to sound normal. She wanted to sob, to cry, to rail at the fates, but for now, she was going to hold herself up stoically. "Now, what?"

"There will be an investigation–" he began and then her phone rang. Without hesitation, he answered it for her. She watched in surprise as he said, "Hello?" He paused to listen. "No, no comment. No comment....No, no comment." He must have said 'no comment' at least half a dozen times before he hung up the phone.

"You don't want me to talk to the media?" she asked, staring at the water in her cup as she realized who must have been on the phone.

"It would be better if you didn't," he advised.

She nodded to show she understood. The phone rang again. She glanced up as he answered it again. This time, he seemed to know the person on the other end.

"Yeah?" A long while seemed to pass as he listened. "I've got it handled," he told the unknown caller and then hung up.

"You said you are from the union?" she asked, becoming more aware, wakening from what had been an almost dream-like state.

"I'm sorry. I didn't properly introduce myself. I'm Andy Warhowicz."

"You're a pilot too?" she asked, glancing at his wings again.

He nodded, realizing how observant she was.

"Do they know what happened yet?"

"I don't know," he admitted, still watching her.

She pierced him with a look. "You knew enough to come to my home."

He nodded, admitting she was right. "They wanted me here before the media arrived and surprised you."

She nodded, grateful for the consideration, but it didn't change the dilemma she found herself in.

"Is there any chance that she…?" she began, seeking out all options.

"All we do know is, there was some type of explosion."

She looked up again, this time staring at the ceiling as if seeking answers there. "How many were on board?"

"Two hundred," he told her sorrowfully.

Oh, gawd. Two hundred souls plus the crew all gone! "Where were they?"

"They were beginning their descent into Belgium," he explained.

"Land or sea?"

"Excuse me?"

"Did the crash occur over land or sea?"

"In the sea."

She nodded, realizing most would have frozen in those deep waters even if they had survived the explosion. She swallowed the sob that wanted to leak out. "You will have to excuse me," she told him. "Help yourself to anything in the kitchen," she offered, pointing to the cereal and coffee maker as she turned.

He watched as she shuffled off towards the stairs. He could already hear the sobs she had been trying so valiantly to hold back. Shrugging off his trench coat, he revealed his suit with the captain's wings on his

lapel, which showed that he too was a full-fledged pilot. Laying his coat on the counter, he looked around, then following her steps to the stairwell, he glanced up. He heard her climbing the stairs and heard the already familiar creaking of the floor above his head before silence once again descended on the remote house. He no longer heard her muffled cries, the ones she wouldn't release in front of him, and now, the house was dark. Searching, he found a light panel and flipped a couple switches. Lights went on in both the living room and what looked like a den across the hall. He chose to look in the den, curious about this couple.

The den was decorated warmly with maple wood and matching leather couches and chairs. A desk stood in one corner, facing out of the room with a leather chair behind it. The leather of the desk chair matched the couches and chairs. It was all tastefully done. He remembered the dossier on this pilot said her wife was a decorator. He approved. The room was very inviting. He looked at the shelves, admiring the hardbacks and the pictures showing two women. The woman whose life he had just turned upside down, a brunette, and the other, a dark blonde whose death had shattered their seemingly picture-perfect life. Standing between the women in one picture was a little girl, obviously the daughter of both women with her red-brown hair and a nose that matched the dead woman's facial features. He sat down on the couch next to an end table with a phone, wondering about the two women's lives together as he fielded calls and repeated, "No comment," at least one-hundred times that night.

TO BE CONTINUED...

About the Author

K'Anne Meinel is a Lesbian Fiction bestselling author with more than 100 published works including shorts, novellas, and novels. She is an American author born in Milwaukee, Wisconsin and raised in Oconomowoc. Upon early graduation from high school she went to a private college in Milwaukee and then moved to California for seventeen years before returning to the state. Many of her stories have Wisconsin in them as settings for her wonderful, realistic, and detailed backgrounds. Named the lesbian Danielle Steel of her time, K'Anne continues to write interesting stories in a variety of genres in both the lesbian and mainstream fiction categories.

What do you do when you meet someone who changes everything you know about love and passion?

Paige Harlow is a good girl. She's always known where she was going in life: top grades, an ivy league school, a medical degree, regular church attendance, and a happy marriage to a man. So falling in love with her gorgeous roommate and best friend Alyssa Torres is no small crisis. Alyssa is chasing demons of her own, a medical condition that makes her an outcast and a family dysfunctional to the point of disintegration make her a questionable choice for any stable relationship. But Paige's heart is no longer her own. She must now battle the prejudices of her family, friends, and church and come to peace with her new sexuality before she can hope to win the affections of the woman of her dreams. But will love be enough?

www.shadoepublishing.com

When Delaney Delacroix is called to locate a missing girl, she never plans on getting caught up with a human trafficking investigation or with the local witch. Meeting with Raelin Montrose changes her life in so many ways that Delaney isn't sure that this isn't destiny.

Raelin Montrose is a practicing Wiccan, and when the ley lines that run under her home tell her that someone is coming, she can't imagine that she was going to solve a mystery and find the love of her life at the same time.

~ Because a publisher should stand behind their authors~

Amelia Gittens had the credit of being the first and only woman thus far in the United States military of being a sniper in combat, made possible by being in the Military Police unit of the crack 10th Mountain Infantry Division. After retirement she joins the City of New York Police Department, and suddenly finds herself involved in a suspect shooting incident which soon encroaches upon her entire life. In order to protect her therapist who has been targeted as a revenge killing, Amelia takes on the responsibility as if she was still in the Army, treating it as a tactical maneuver.

www.shadoepublishing.com

~ Because a publisher should stand behind their authors~

An abused and bullied teenager is suddenly granted great and terrible powers by an ancient goddess. Each step towards womanhood is shaped by her new abilities, as is the woman she will become. Devil or angel, which will she be? Will the woman who chases her ever know for sure?

Both men tried to shoot her then, and the two women were stunned at the speed with which she moved. Penny charged straight at the gunmen then dove under their fire. Spinning on her back she kicked the legs from under one man, and as he fell, she kicked the gun from the other man's hand. Spinning back to the first man she saw the gun barrel moving toward her, and she lashed out with her foot. Her boot crushed his skull and she rolled to her feet to grab the last man in a neck lock. A quick twist and he lay lifeless in her arms.

She let him fall, as, breathing deeply, she came down off combat mode. "Are you ladies all right?" she asked as she untied the ropes that held the older woman.

"Who are you?" asked the old woman fearfully, as she pulled the tape from her mouth.

"They call me Lady Blue," smiled Penny as she helped the woman to stand.

"What are you?" It was the younger woman who spoke.

"Cold, hungry, dead tired, and covered in blue war paint," giggled Penny as she released the older woman's arm. She turned and began to search the bodies.